HAUNTED U.S. BATTLEFIELDS

Ghosts, Hauntings, and Eerie Events
from America's Fields of Honor

Mary Beth Crain

D1053803

Copyright © 2008 by Mary Beth Crain

Designed by Sheryl P. Kober

Library of Congress Cataloging-in-Publication Data is available on file.

ISBN 978-0-7627-4936-2

Printed in the United States of America

10 9 8 7 6 5 4 3 2

To all the battlefield ghosts—it's been great meeting you, and may you someday make it back home.

CONTENTS

ACKNOWLEDGMENTS

There are just a few people to whom I'd like to say, "Thanks, guys, I couldn't have done it without you!"

My editor, Mary Norris, who somehow always believed I could do this project faster than the speed of light.

My project manager, Jennifer Taber, who did a super job pulling it all together.

My witty and loving cousin, Claire Bucalos, who provided critical humor breaks.

My dear friends, Brenda Bont and Roger Simkins, who babysat my whining, neglected Chihuahua, Truman, during the frantic last laps of my deadline.

And, of course, John Spalding—awesome editor, awesome writer, and, above all, awesome friend.

INTRODUCTION

Since ancient times, tales of battlefield spirits and ghosts have been a part of lore and legend. In the days before TV and computers, they made for good stories and not much more. But today, with the aid of the sophisticated ghost-busting gear we see on shows like *Ghost Hunters* and *America's Most Haunted,* and at paranormal research centers around the world, it's not nearly so easy to pooh-pooh the existence of the supernatural. Strange figures and shapes can be seen floating and flickering on video; strange sounds and voices groan and crackle on state-of-the-art voice-detection equipment. Intrepid men and women bravely venture into haunted territory, determined to prove the existence of ghosts. Sometimes they're disappointed; sometimes they end up fleeing in screaming terror.

When it comes to haunted territory, battlefields are pretty much sure bets. Sites of extreme violence and emotion, battlefields contain all the ingredients for a good old-fashioned ghost sighting. With so many lives cut painfully short, and so many bodies left to disintegrate, unrecognized and unconsecrated, it's no wonder restless, anguished spirits wander the tragic soil, in search of . . . what? Peace? Closure? A chance to have their final say?

Battlefield ghosts have many reasons for hanging around. Sudden death, especially at a young age, can thrust ghosts into a kind of time warp, where they can't quite grasp the reality of their altered state. It's said that many spirits don't know they're dead, and need help to navigate in their new surroundings. Psychics are often their tour guides, providing a road map and a good kick in the rear that sends these confused souls barreling into "the light."

Or a battlefield ghost may refuse to go gently into that light. Perhaps it's stubborn, and determined to remain earthbound. Or it may have a grudge against someone on Earth, a score to settle, and it won't leave until vengeance has been exacted. In other cases, a ghost may be searching for something or someone, disconsolately roaming the earth in a state of endless yearning and grief, as it vainly tries to contact a relative or lost love.

As dreadful as battlefields are, they are also places of high energy and enthusiasm. For many young men, war was the defining moment of their lives. To a boy of seventeen, eighteen, twenty, who had hardly been out of his own backyard before he was rudely thrust onto the front, a battle was undoubtedly the most exciting thing that had ever happened to him. It was a rite of passage, his ticket to manhood. It gave him a mission, a sense of identity, a devotion to a higher purpose, the reward for which was something he could never have earned back on the boring farm or in the quiet old hometown: glory. So some battlefield ghosts may not want to leave the premises simply because they're still fighting. They've become so addicted to the "high" of battle that they reenact, over and over, the events that gave them such a rush.

Finally, ghosts—and in particular battlefield ghosts— often haunt an area because they've got something important to say. There might be last words that were never heard, facts about a death or murder that were never known, a message to their wives, girlfriends, or other loved ones that they feel they must impart before they can comfortably exit terra firma.

Haunted U.S. Battlefields is a compilation of stories about supernatural events associated with these violent sites. From the battlefields of the Revolutionary War and the Civil War to those of the two world wars and other military conflicts, the dead have refused to let go of the past. In the following pages, you'll learn about famous spirits and apparitions, such as the "Ghost Rider of Little Round Top," who allegedly turned the tide of the Civil War; "Old Green Eyes," a weird creature who takes various chilling forms at the notorious Chickamauga Battlefield; the "Faceless Phantom of Corregidor," a terrifying entity who haunts a hotel on the infamous "Island of Death" in the Philippines that claimed so many American lives during World War II; the "Ghosts of the Bloody Lane" of Antietam, who for the past 146 years have been replaying scenes of battle in a creepy continuous loop; and many more.

You don't believe in ghosts? Hmm. After reading this book, you just might change your mind. At any rate, enjoy it—and keep the light on.

Part One

THE FRENCH AND INDIAN WAR

Chapter 1

Ticonderoga and the Haunting of Duncan Campbell

*This is the tale of the man
Who heard a word in the night
In the land of the heathery hills,
In the days of the feud and the fight.
By the sides of the rainy sea,
Where never a stranger came,
On the awful lips of the dead,
He heard the outlandish name.
It sang in his sleeping ears,
It hummed in his waking head:
The name—Ticonderoga,
The utterance of the dead.*

*From "Ticonderoga: A Legend of the West Highlands,"
by Robert Louis Stevenson*

Fort Ticonderoga was a key stronghold during the French and Indian War. Located at the strategic intersection of Lake Champlain and Lake George in upstate New York, the fortification controlled frequently used trade routes between the English-controlled Hudson River Valley and the French-controlled Saint Lawrence River Valley. "Ticonderoga" comes from an Iroquois word meaning "at the junction of two waterways." It's a name that would be well known to the American Indians—but certainly not to the Scottish Highlanders in 1750. Yet in one of the spookiest ghost tales that arose out of the French and Indian War, the name Ticonderoga is linked to a terrible premonition that involved Duncan Campbell, Lord of Inverawe and major of the 42nd Regiment of Foot, also known as the Royal Highlanders, or the Black Watch.

The story begins in Scotland in 1755, several years before the outbreak of the war. Was it a "dark and stormy night"? Probably. The western Highlands are known for their wild beauty, and the rain might very well have been lashing at the windows as Lord Campbell sat in the old hall of his ancient castle of Inverawe, on the banks of the Awe, on that all too memorable evening when the dead and the living were scheduled to collide in a fateful rendezvous.

Campbell, according to those who knew him, was a good, kind, God-fearing sort, known for his integrity and loyalty. So when he heard a banging at the door and, upon opening it, beheld a man in torn clothing and a blood-drenched kilt, out of breath and clearly panicked, he ignored caution and immediately invited the visitor inside.

"Gently, man, gently," said Campbell, trying to calm the agitated man. "Who are ye, now?"

"They are after me!" the stranger gasped. "Close the door! Will you shelter me for the night?"

"And what have ye done?" inquired Campbell.

"I have killed a man."

While most would, at this point, have excused themselves to seek refuge, Campbell remained gracious as usual.

"Murder, is it?" He nodded. "Well, it's not the first time murder's been done in Scotland. Had ye a guid cause?"

"As good a cause as any man has ever had," the stranger fervently replied. "Now, will you hide me?"

"No man has ever claimed hospitality of me without receiving it," good Lord Campbell assured him, never suspecting that those words would haunt him forever.

"Promise me you'll tell no one of my presence," the stranger begged. Campbell promised. But the stranger was not satisfied.

"Swear on your dirk!" he insisted.

To swear on one's dirk, or dagger, was the ultimate test of Celtic honor. Campbell swore and then led the fugitive to a secret recess in the depths of the castle. Soon there was another loud knocking at the door. This time it was two armed men.

"Your cousin Donald has been murdered," one of the men informed Campbell. "We are looking for his killer."

"I have seen no one," said Campbell, and the men left.

Now the Lord of Inverawe was deeply torn, his loyalties divided between his dead cousin and the man who murdered him. He lay down to rest in a large, dark room but was awakened sometime during the night by the bloody and perturbed ghost of his cousin, Donald Campbell.

"Inverawe! Inverawe!" declared the fearful apparition, in hollow, ominous tones. "Blood has been shed! Shield not the murderer!"

Campbell didn't waste any time. Jumping out of bed, he ran to the murderer's hiding place and told him he could no longer grant him asylum. Now he had two disgruntled visitors.

"You have sworn on your dirk!" the stranger reminded him. "Woe to him who breaks this oath!"

Duncan Campbell stood in front of the stranger, betwixt and between. If he broke the oath, he would suffer not only eternal shame but possibly death at the hands of his insulted guest. If he honored it, he risked the wrath of a wraith. Trying to strike a compromise, Campbell ushered the murderer to a cave in a nearby mountain and left him there, reiterating his promise not to divulge his whereabouts.

The following night he was once again awakened by his cousin's ghost, who repeated the previous night's warning. "Inverawe! Inverawe! Blood has been shed! Shield not the murderer!"

Campbell hurriedly dressed and ran to the cave. But it was empty and the stranger had vanished. Campbell was vastly relieved; no one could accuse him of shielding anyone now. Hopefully his ghostly night caller would be satisfied.

But nay. That night, dead cousin Donald appeared once more, this time with a portentous, if cryptic, message. "Farewell, Inverawe!" he intoned. "Farewell, till we meet once more at Ticonderoga!" Then the spirit turned and vanished.

Ticonderoga? Where or what was Ticonderoga? Mystified, Campbell gave up trying to figure out the ghost's message. But the strange-sounding word remained in his memory.

Three years later, in 1758, Duncan Campbell, now a major in the Black Watch, the regiment assigned to keep order in the turbulent Highlands, journeyed with his men to America to join the British forces under General James Abercrombie in the French and Indian War. One old tale describes the stirring scene of the Black Watch on the march:

Abercrombie commanded the British and the Provincials. They were camped down at Albany, and then they marched northward. It was a braw sight, with the Black Watch in front, their pipers in the bright red Stewart tartan bravely skirling Cock o' the North, and the white gaiters of a thousand men swinging along beneath the dark cloud that was the twelve-yard Black Watch plaid. . . . And northward they marched in the summertime, and the hearts of the countryfolk were gay because this was the Army that would end the depredations of the savage Indians and the fierce Frenchmen.

The battle plan was to attack the French bastion of Fort Carillon. At a village along the way, the 42nd Regiment stopped at an inn. A pretty young girl struck up a conversation with Major Campbell. As the men were about to leave, she said, "Will you be coming back this way? After you take Ticonderoga?"

Campbell stood there in shock, agape. "Ticonderoga?" he stammered. "But they said we are to attack Fort Carillon."

"Oh, that's what the French call it," the girl explained. "But the Indian name is Ticonderoga."

As soon as he heard this, Campbell knew he was doomed. His brother officers, all of whom had heard the tale of the major's ghostly visitor and his fateful promise, tried to calm him with well-meaning trickery. When they reached their destination on the eve of the battle, they argued with him that since the military considered the place Fort Carillon, the name Ticonderoga should be ignored. The following morning, however, an exhausted Campbell emerged from his tent, looking haggard and resigned.

"I have seen him," he murmured. "He came to my tent last night. This is Ticonderoga, and I shall die today!"

The morning of July 8, 1758, General Abercrombie staged a frontal attack outside Fort Ticonderoga's main walls. Attempting to move as quickly as possible, Abercrombie decided to forgo field cannons in favor of sheer manpower. But his sixteen thousand troops were no match for the mere four thousand French defenders, who soundly routed the invader. Among the worst hit were the men of the 42nd Regiment of Foot, who suffered massive casualties—one of whom was Major Duncan Campbell. His arm shattered by a bullet, Campbell was carried to Fort Edward. His arm was amputated, but he lived only a few days more. On the stone that marks his grave at Fort Ticonderoga is the epitaph:

Here lyes the Body of Duncan Campbell of Inverawe, Esquire, Major to the old Highland Regiment, aged 55 years, who died the 17th of July, 1758, of the Wounds he received in the Attack of the Retrenchment of Ticonderoga on the 8th of July, 1758.

But Donald Campbell wasn't the only member of the Campbell clan to appear in death to his relatives. On the day Major Campbell died, it is believed his spirit crossed an ocean to bid a last farewell to his foster brother. Many years later, in the 1880s, the then–Lord of Inverawe related the tale:

"I knew an old man whose grandfather was foster brother to the slain Major of the 42nd, and who told me the following story. The old man's grandfather was sleeping with his young son—the narrator's father—in the same room, but in another bed. The boy was awakened by some unaccustomed sound, and behold—there was a bright light in the room. The boy then saw a figure, in full Highland regimentals, cross over the room and stoop down over his father's bed and give him a kiss. The lad was too frightened to speak but hid instead under his coverlet until he fell asleep. In the morning he spoke to his father about it. The older man told him that it was 'Macdonnochie' [the Gaelic patronymic of the Lord of Inverawe] whom he had seen, and who came to tell him that he had been killed in a great battle in America. Sure enough, said my informant, it was on that very day that the Laird died of the wounds he suffered at Ticonderoga."

And so, like the ghosts that inspired it, the legend of the haunting of Duncan Campbell refuses to die. It just gets better as time goes on. We'll let Robert Louis Stevenson conclude the story:

And it fell on the morrow's morning,
In the fiercest of the fight,
That Duncan Campbell bit the dust
As he foretold at night;
And far from the hills of heather
Far from the isles of the sea,
He sleeps in the place of the name
As it was doomed to be.

Chapter 2
The Ghosts of
Beardslee Castle

In the beautiful Mohawk Valley, Beardslee Castle stands as a testament to the presence of the undead. It's said to be a favorite playground for all manner of ghosts, in particular the Native Americans who inhabited the region and who, during the French and Indian War, experienced a trauma on the grounds that may have been the beginning of the Indians' war with the Beardslees.

In a picturesque area of upstate New York, elegant old Beardslee Castle welcomes visitors from all over the world. They come not only for the cuisine and the hospitality, but also for the chance to experience one of the many ghost sightings for which the restaurant has become famous.

Although Beardslee Castle dates from 1860, the land on which it was built is far older. Just to the east of the castle is the site of what was once a major Mohawk camp that dated from the 1400s. In the mid-eighteenth century, during the French and Indian War, the Mohawk Valley was the central supply point for militias along the northern borders of the colonies and was of critical strategic importance to both the British, who used it as a corridor to the Great Lakes, from which to attack New France directly, and to the French, for whom it was a corridor to the Hudson Valley and the heart of British North America.

A fortified homestead that was a storage house for munitions and powder stood on the property where the castle is now located, in Little Falls, New York. One night, the story goes, a band of Indians broke into the home to steal the munitions. But their torches ignited the powder and the intruders blew themselves up. Their spirits, many maintain, haunt the castle to this day, along with the ghosts of other peeved Native Americans. Psychic researchers who have visited the castle agree on the presence of some sort of restless spirit energy on the premises and believe that it is somehow linked to the Indians who long inhabited the region.

Augustus Beardslee built his impressive estate just before the Civil War. His son, Guy Beardslee, graduated from West Point in 1879 and spent time in North Dakota, fighting the Sioux. He returned to New York with many trophies of his exploits, among which were Indian war bonnets, tomahawks, knives, and other ceremonial artifacts. The Sioux hold sacred such artifacts of war, but Beardslee apparently didn't have much respect for these items, which might explain why unfortunate things began occurring at the castle. As the castle's Web site notes, the mere presence of these artifacts "could have profound effects, especially if they had been taken in battle."

Another way in which Guy Beardslee may not have endeared himself to Native American spirits concerned the part he played in bringing electricity to the Mohawk Valley. In 1892 he was paid $40,000 to harness the waterfalls in the area for electric power. He thus is credited with building the first rural electrification plant in the United States. What the white man saw as a boon to civilization, however, would have come under the classification of supreme bad luck to the local Mohawks, who regarded the waterfalls with awe, as a manifestation of the Great Spirit on earth. Guy Beardslee's meddling with nature undoubtedly would have been seen as nothing less than sacrilege.

In 1919 Beardslee was vacationing in Florida when the castle mysteriously caught fire. The cause was never determined, but all of the Sioux war artifacts were destroyed in the blaze. Of course, it could have been just one of those things. On the other hand, the incident seems to have a place in the long list of disturbing events that have been reported in and around the castle ever since.

After the fire, the castle was restored. Beardslee died in 1937, and in 1946 Anton "Pop" Christensen and his wife purchased the property and turned it into a restaurant. In the 1950s Pop Christensen became terminally ill. One tragic day, his body was found in the ladies' room. Despondent over his illness, he had hanged himself. Soon thereafter, inexplicable things began happening at the castle. It began with simple mischief—kitchen utensils being misplaced immediately after they had been set, glassware moved around, items taken out of cupboards and relocated to other spots.

But then mischief escalated to malevolence. Employees arrived in the morning to find chairs and tables overturned. Some insisted they'd seen silverware flying through the air. Bottles and glasses exploded with no provocation. Noises with no discernable source could be heard throughout the building. Water turned on and off by itself. One night, half in jest, several employees decided to try to contact the "ghosts" with the aid of a Ouija board. At one point the board spelled out "L-E-A-V-E." Then the lights went out. And then one of the participants got a good dose of genuine spirit wrath.

"I felt physically assaulted by some invisible force," he reported. "It hit me in the chest and pushed me clear across the room. Then it knocked me to the floor." The Ouija enthusiasts needed no further encouragement. They fled the castle.

Several years later, hostess Cherrie Fox and two other restaurant employees experienced similar ghostly inhospitality. They were closing up for the night and were just about to go into the back room to turn off the lights when Fox said, "There's somebody in there." The three turned back and returned to the bar. That was when they heard the sound—a sound, Fox said, that was positively nonhuman. "It was the combination of a shriek and a growl. It was so loud it seemed to come from all around us." The unearthly utterance propelled the three employees up the stairs and out of the castle. As in the case of the Ouija players, a sinister presence obviously wanted these three to "L-E-A-V-E"— A-S-A-P.

At around the time of these occurrences, the castle's owner invited Norm Gauthier, an investigator from the New Hampshire Institute for Paranormal Research, and some forty reporters from various media to a ghost hunting party. Armed with EVP equipment and incense, Gauthier proceeded to test the premises for paranormal activity. At the end of the night, when the tapes were played back, faint whispery voices could be heard. There was no sign, however, of any irritation on the part of the spirits; in fact, some sounded almost playful—as if they were delighted to have media attention at last. Gauthier's expert conclusion? The castle was haunted by at least two spirits.

Could one of those spirits be "Abigail," the young woman many people have described as dressed in white, wandering the grounds or standing in windows? Supposedly, Abigail was a bride who died the night before her wedding at the castle, in the days when it was still a residence. Several psychics have reported encountering a young woman in a white satin dress with a high collar and long sleeves. Perhaps the most convincing evidence of Abigail's presence, though, was the account of a visitor who was completely unfamiliar with both the property and its attendant ghost stories. This witness not only described the "lady in white"—she actually had some detailed information about her. The young woman, she said, was "fond of fabrics, flowers, and most of all, the castle. She's still here because she loved the place so much."

Others have seen a young child walking along the road-side late at night. And then there are the supposed sight-ings of Guy Beardslee himself, walking the grounds holding a lantern with a blue light and searching for a lost child who had been killed. The lantern has been witnessed by numerous people, including one of Pop Christensen's grand-daughters, who said she saw it floating on its own behind the castle.

In the 1950s, immediately following Pop Christensen's suicide, the phenomenon of the "evil lights" began. Travel-ers along Route 5 reported seeing a blinding blue or yellow light that would burst from the trees, chasing them down the road. The light was the cause of a number of fatal acci-dents. One woman who survived a crash that killed her hus-band described the event. "The light rushed out from the trees and blinded my husband. The car went off the road and crashed into a tree." The unexplained lights have been around for years. The newest owners of the castle report that "in the past six years since the castle reopened, we have had four incidents of cars driving off the road in a per-fectly clear, straight stretch less than a quarter-mile long in front of the castle."

One accident in particular still has everyone baffled, including the police. A couple was traveling past the castle when a young woman stepped out into the road. Unable to stop in time, they hit her. Horrified, they got out of the car and rushed to the victim—only to find no one there. Fortunately, there were witnesses in a car traveling in the opposite direction. They backtracked to the scene and were also mystified. Yes, they insisted, we saw her. She walked right out in front of you. We saw the whole thing.

When the police arrived, everyone scoured the area, searching for a body. But they never found anyone. And there were no marks on the car.

Eerie disturbances became part of life at the castle. Staff routinely refused to go upstairs alone and unanimously deemed certain rooms more haunted than others. Weird noises were everywhere. Music was sometimes heard floating down from the second floor, along with the sound of a woman singing. There was the frequent sound of muttering, and a number of employees heard their names sharply whispered, as though from a fellow staff member. But when they looked around, there was never anyone there. There were the sounds of doors opening and closing. Employees reported hearing footsteps across the main hall—after everyone had left the dining rooms.

And then there are the photographs. Strange rainbows that don't conform to the traditional light spectrum, ghostly mists and auras, orbs, and other phenomena have appeared in photos taken throughout the castle and in the mausoleum where the Beardslee deceased are buried. The most convincing shot, however, was taken by a former staff member who decided to snap some pictures of his old haunts, no pun intended. When he had the film developed, the form of a shadowy figure with an expression of alarm covered the entire frame. The photo was declared authentic by the producer of television's *Haunted History*, who, in his many travels to haunted locations throughout the country, had been shown hundreds of such images. But this one, he said, was "the best I've ever seen—bar none."

And it seems the Native Americans might still have a score to settle with the Beardslees. In 1989, seventy years after the castle mysteriously burned down in 1919, fire again struck the building. It supposedly started in the kitchen, in the early hours of the morning. Again, the cause was undetermined, and there was no one in the kitchen at the time. At the same time, water pipes inexplicably burst in the basement and continued to leak for three years.

A psychic living in New York City did a long-distance "reading" on the castle and pinpointed the disruptive and eerie activity in the exact sites employees and patrons had described. The most haunted areas were those where water was present, particularly where water problems had plagued the building. Could this have anything to do with the Native American belief in water as the dwelling place of spirits? Perhaps if Guy Beardslee hadn't tampered with those waterfalls, the castle might be ghost-free. Today we're complaining about the skyrocketing costs of electricity. But could it be that back in 1892, when the lights first went on at Beardslee Castle, the price of electricity was far higher than anyone could know?

Part Two

THE REVOLUTIONARY WAR

Chapter 3

Patrick Ferguson: Ghost King of the Mountain?

Commanding officers are not by nature humble. But Lieutenant Colonel Patrick Ferguson stands out in American history as one of the most arrogant. Yet in Ferguson's case, pride went before a big fall—defeat and death in the Battle of King's Mountain. Was Ferguson so humiliated that to this day he remains on the battlefield, refusing to believe he could have been wrong?

Patrick Ferguson's grave sits atop King's Mountain National Military Park in North Carolina. The fallen Scotsman's remains were once the subject of controversy; Ferguson, a British officer in the Revolutionary War, was known for his unbridled contempt for the Americans, and after his death on the battlefield of King's Mountain, the Patriots stripped his body bare and took turns urinating on it. Then they hastily buried him in a shallow grave atop the mountain, his corpse protected only by a pile of rocks.

Many years later, local Scots, their hearts still firmly with the Patriot cause, began nonetheless to feel some remorse over the degrading treatment their kinsman had received. According to Celtic tradition, they began piling more rocks on Ferguson's grave, giving the old soldier a true Scottish cairn, or rock burial.

But Ferguson, they say, isn't in his cairn. Oh, no. Not the feisty Scotsman with the sharp wit, mischievous smile, and haughty pride of a loyal subject of the British Empire. He always said he wouldn't be caught dead on enemy ground. And apparently he meant it.

In his book *The Winning of the West,* Theodore Roosevelt called the Battle of King's Mountain "the turning point of the American Revolution." Indeed, the bloody clash between Patriot and Loyalist forces resulted in an unexpected and much-needed victory for the bold but ragtag army of Americans who did all they could to hold their own against their more experienced and better equipped opponents.

In the summer of 1790, General Charles Cornwallis embarked on a campaign to capture South Carolina, North Carolina, and finally Virginia, the wealthiest of the southern states. This would assure Britain control of the South's three major coastal colonies.

Cornwallis was victorious in South Carolina, although the southern Over Mountain men proved to be tough adversaries. The early frontiersmen got their name because they'd come over the mountain from what is now Tennessee and southwest Virginia to do their part in the Patriot cause. Unlike the British, they were a volunteer army under self-appointed commanders who were experts in the art of hit-and-run guerrilla raids that proved so annoying to the enemy in the backwoods of the South.

The British, however, were not impressed with the persistence of the gritty frontiersmen. They regarded them with disdain, as savages pure and simple, who sooner or later would have no choice but to surrender to superior British intelligence and skill.

And no one held the backwoods battalions in more contempt than Colonel Patrick Ferguson. Dismissing them as "backwater barbarians," Ferguson was convinced that they were of no more concern to his army than a pack of flies was to a herd of elephants. Pesky, perhaps, but ultimately harmless.

Ferguson was a fascinating fellow. Born in Aberdeenshire, Scotland, in 1744, he was already a commissioned officer at the age of only fifteen. Although Ferguson is most famous for his military exploits, you'll find him listed in the annals of noteworthy Scottish inventors; he developed the breech-loading rifle, a vast improvement over the British Brown Bess muzzle-loading musket. The Ferguson rifle, as it was called, was capable of firing a then-astounding seven shots a minute and could be loaded and fired when the soldier was supine and not in a standing position, reducing his exposure to enemy fire. Although it was Cornwallis's superior military strategy and Washington's strategic blundering that ultimately defeated the Americans at Brandywine in 1777, the Ferguson rifle also played its part in the British victory.

A man of incredible resolve and stubbornness, Ferguson ironically was done in by the very qualities that made him a good commander. It's great to be unyielding on the battlefield, but it's not so helpful when you're dealing with the sensitive, volatile issues that involve hearts and emotions.

While Cornwallis was engaged in South Carolina, he put Ferguson in command of the Loyalist militia, to protect his western flank. Ferguson went into the hills to recruit and train Loyalist sympathizers. Here, his arrogance toward the enemy worked against him. In a celebrated tactical blunder, Ferguson sent an ultimatum to Over Mountain leader Isaac

Shelby, informing him and other Patriot officers that if they didn't lay down their arms, he would march his army over the Blue Ridge Mountains, "hang your leaders and lay your country waste with fire and sword."

Unfortunately, this ominous proclamation backfired. Ferguson had seriously underestimated the Over Mountain men's fierce sense of honor and allegiance to the cause of freedom. Instead of being impressed by the conceited Scotsman's threat, the Patriots grew firmer in their resolve. The infamous ultimatum turned out to be a powerful recruiting tool for the enemy it was supposed to have terrified.

By the time he made his way into North Carolina, Ferguson was so hated by the Americans that his very name engendered immediate rage. This burning emotion would transform into the white-hot energy of revenge when the Over Mountain men finally came face to face with their nemesis at King's Mountain.

Cornwallis reached Charlotte, North Carolina, on September 26, 1790. On October 1, Ferguson committed his second, and even more heinous, tactical blunder. Arrogance unabated, he issued what was to become his notorious "Address to the People of North Carolina," in which he declared in pungent, if ungrammatical, tones:

> Gentlemen: Unless you wish to be eat up by an inundation of barbarians . . . you wish to be pinioned, robbed, and murdered, and see your wives and daughters . . . abused by the dregs of mankind . . . grasp your arms in a moment and run to camp. The Back Water men have crossed the mountains; McDowell, Hampton, Shelby and Cleveland are at their head . . . If you choose to be degraded forever

and ever by a set of mongrels, say so at once and let your women turn upon you, and look for real men to protect them!

Again, the warning had the opposite of its intended effect. Ferguson hoped to scare the populace into the arms of the British. Instead, it was a victory for the "mongrels." There was a huge scramble to join up with Colonels Charles McDowell and Isaac Shelby. When Ferguson reached King's Mountain, he was at a disadvantage.

The Patriots planned to surround the base of the mountain and wait for Ferguson to come to them. But even though Ferguson knew of their strategy, having gotten the scoop from a captured deserter, he refused to take his adversary seriously. He proudly lined up his men along the top of the long, spoon-shaped ridge, certain that the inhospitable landscape of thick trees and boulders would block the advance of the "barbarians." But the Appalachian frontiersmen Ferguson had so incensed were just as rugged as the terrain. Not only did they outnumber his forces—but they also knew the mountain territory inside and out, a distinct advantage over the enemy.

What Ferguson had laughed at in the Over Mountain men—their lack of military discipline and experience—turned out to be their ace in the hole. The scrappy band of Patriot volunteers might not have had the training and skill of the Loyalist forces, but then, they weren't battlefield soldiers. They were Indian fighters, most comfortable in the rough wilderness that Ferguson wrongly assumed would thwart them.

So on the morning of October 7, as Ferguson's troops stood proudly and stiffly atop the ridge, boots polished, sabers shining, and red coats blazing, the motley Americans made their way up King's Mountain, nimbly scampering around the trees and rocks that provided a perfect natural shield against enemy fire. They responded to the British volley like the seasoned snipers they were. And, like sitting ducks, Ferguson's men began toppling over where they stood. By the time the surprised colonel finally realized his tactics weren't working, it was too late. He gave the classic, "Bayonets! Charge!" order, and what was left of his troops raced down the mountain, bayonets thrust forward. But the Patriots simply retreated, disappearing into the dense woods.

"Resume positions!" barked Ferguson, with inexplicable stupidity. Dutifully, the British marched right back up the mountain, to take up their old position atop the ridge, whereupon the Over Mountain men popped up from their hiding places and hit them with sniper fire all over again.

We mentioned that Ferguson was stubborn. Unable to get it through his head that his men were being slaughtered, he ordered another charge down the mountain! Naturally, the same ritual was repeated. The Loyalists charged, the Patriots vanished into the trees, the Loyalists went back up the mountain, and the Patriots shot them down from the vantage point of their shielded positions.

It didn't take long for white flags to begin fluttering along Ferguson's line. But the dogged colonel, still contemptuous of his low-class opponent, refused to admit defeat. Galloping astride his white stallion, Ferguson rode along his line, commanding his beleaguered troops to continue fighting, and tearing the white handkerchiefs and shirts out of their hands with the sharp point of his saber. In a last, desperate act of manic fervor, Ferguson gathered up a squad of soldiers and charged down the slope, right into the hands of the barbarians. As his men looked on in horror, the titan of the tartan toppled from his horse, dead, his chest torn open by a volley of musket balls.

King's Mountain was a key victory for the Patriots, and the first major loss for the British in the South. The reason Theodore Roosevelt and other historians hailed it as the turning point of the Revolution was that it was the most important factor in the southern colonies' decision to join their northern compatriots in the pursuit of independence.

Although the Patriots gleefully desecrated Ferguson's body, history has been kinder to him. Today, alongside his burial cairn, a statue stands commemorating the valor of this crusty Scotsman. Erected on top of King's Mountain by the U.S. government in 1930, on the 150th anniversary of the battle, the monument reads, COL. PATRICK FERGUSON. A SOLDIER OF MILITARY DISTINCTION AND HONOR. It seems as though Ferguson appreciated this noble, if belated, gesture of decency, because, as the stories go, his ghost began appearing at his statue soon afterward. And then people began spotting him all over the old battlefield.

Visitors to King's Mountain National Military Park have reported seeing him at dusk, heading toward the top of the mountain astride his white horse, his red coat flashing through the trees. But whenever onlookers try to follow the figure, it vanishes into the approaching darkness. Ferguson makes a more solid appearance, however, at his cairn and his statue. Tourists at these spots say they have seen him materialize right before their eyes. He looks just like he does in his portraits, in full battle uniform, eyes twinkling with a bit of the old Scotch mischief, smiling slightly, as though he's pleased as punch to be recognized. The apparition never remains for long; usually it's gone before observers realize just what they've seen.

One amazing sighting of Ferguson concerns two Revolutionary War enthusiasts who actually had the nerve to take a nighttime stroll through the battlefield. They were standing in front of the cairn, they reported, when Ferguson actually came out of the shadows and stood staring at them from just a few feet away. Then he spoke, they swear. In a thick Scottish brogue he said, "Cairns don't always keep the spirits of the dead from wandering!" Then he roared with laughter, walked back toward the woods, and disappeared. Was it his ghost, or someone dressed up as the colonel and playing a joke? The witnesses firmly believe it was Ferguson, not only because he so resembled his portrait, but also because of the way he vanished—in classic apparition form, fading away into thin air. On the other hand, it was dark. But on the other hand . . .

There's a postscript to King's Mountain. In the centuries following the American Revolution, a story has arisen that Ferguson's ghost has been seen in Wilkes County, North Carolina. According to local folklorist R. G. Absher, "Following the battle of King's Mountain, Col. Benjamin Cleveland of the North Carolina militia was presented Col. Ferguson's horse as a spoil of war." The white Arabian, says Absher, was Ferguson's most cherished possession, and famous within the British army. Cleveland acquired it because his own mount, Roebuck, was shot from beneath him during the heat of battle. He rode his newly acquired steed back to his plantation home along the Yadkin River on Ronda in the Roundabout.

The horse soon became famous. People would come from all over to see it. After the animal died some years later, sightings began to be reported, of a British officer resembling Ferguson, riding a white horse near the Ronda farm on moonlit nights.

"The officer appeared to be waving his sword," noted Absher. "The horse fit the description of the white Arabian that Ben Cleveland brought back from King's Mountain."

Can ghosts haunt more than one location? Why not? As you'll see in the next chapter, the ghost of "Mad" Anthony Wayne definitely gets around. What seems to be clear is that ghosts return to the spots—however many of them there might be—where there's still something of importance to them. A grave, a statue, a horse—or perhaps a last chance to recover their lost honor.

Chapter 4
The Ghost Rider of Chadds Ford

Many people have witnessed an inexplicable phenomenon in Pennsylvania's Brandywine Valley—a phantom horseman, dressed in the traditional officer's uniform of the Revolutionary War, crossing the Brandywine River or galloping along U.S. Route 1, where the highway intersects with the Brandywine battlefield, glowing with an unearthly light. Who is he, and why does he always seem to be headed north, staring straight ahead with such single-minded determination?

There's an old saying in Chadds Ford, the town in Pennsylvania's Brandywine Valley where Washington defended the Continental Army against the British advance in the Battle of Brandywine. "Beware the autumn nights . . . of full moonlight . . . for that's when he comes . . . the Ghost in White."

It sounds like those corny warnings you find in silly old ghost tales. Only in this case, there's apparently more truth to the jingle than many would like to admit. Numerous people—tourists and residents alike—have reported seeing a phantom rider, dressed in the white breeches, brass-buttoned long blue coat, and tricorner hat of a Continental officer in the Revolutionary War, crossing Chadds Ford on a shining white steed or galloping at breakneck speed through the woods on the east side of the Brandywine River, or along US 1, heading northeast toward Philadelphia.

The mysterious phantom is seen only in the fall, and only by the light of a full moon. Perhaps he wants to be sure nobody misses him as he plows in measured, stately fashion through Chadds Ford, staring straight ahead with lifeless eyes, bathed, along with his horse, in an eerie alabaster glow. Eyewitnesses invariably comment that even though the rider and his steed are moving through the river, their procession is soundless, making not so much as a splash. As one amazed onlooker remarked, "It was like watching a silent movie."

The ghost rider picks up speed in other spots, though. In the Brandywine Valley, he's been sighted tearing through the woods like a streak of white light, as though on some sort of urgent mission. It's on US 1, however, that he causes the most disturbance, wreaking havoc with motorists who swerve to avoid him as he barrels along the middle of the road, eyes still fixed on something in the distance, apparently unaware of anyone else. Yet shaken drivers report that when they pass the galloping eighteenth-century figure, there's no sign of him in their side or rearview mirrors.

Who is this apparition? Well, actually, there seem to be two of them—one intact, the other headless. Witnesses to the latter say he gallops through the valley brandishing his saber. His dress is identical to the other horseman's, with the obvious exception of the three-cornered hat.

Nobody knows who the decapitated horseman might be. The best guess is that he's an unknown casualty of the Battle of Brandywine, still looking for his head. Through the years, however, the identity of the first ghost rider has been narrowed down to none other than "Mad" Anthony Wayne, who, although he was known to have lost his head plenty of times in life, has apparently managed to keep it in the afterlife. The general, who earned his nickname for his fiery personality and daredevil bravado, suffered a crushing defeat at the Battle of Brandywine. Some theorize that he haunts the area in an effort to make amends for his, and General Washington's, mistakes and that the urgent mission that seems to preoccupy him may somehow involve getting information to his commander-in-chief that could turn the tide of the long-lost battle.

In September 1777, the British had their eyes on the prize of Philadelphia, the temporary capital of the newborn United States of America. British General Sir William Howe led the march toward Philadelphia from the Chesapeake, landing at Head of Elk, or what is now Elkton, Maryland.

George Washington was confident that he could stop the enemy in its tracks. He marshaled his defenses on the high ground in the area of Chadds Ford, which allowed safe passage across the Brandywine River on the road from Baltimore to Philadelphia.

On the morning of September 9, Washington positioned his troops along the Brandywine River. This strategy was designed to guard the main fords—Pyles Ford and Wistars Ford—to force a fight at Chadds Ford, where Washington was certain he had the advantage. And a big part of that advantage was his favorite general, "Mad" Anthony Wayne. When it came to pursuing the enemy, Washington knew Wayne would stop at nothing. He could rouse his men to superhuman heights of daring and put the fear of God in anyone who tried to stand in his way.

Wayne's reputation was well known to the British as well. When Howe heard that the feisty Wayne and an entire division of Pennsylvania Continentals would be defending Chadds Ford, he decided against making a play for the strategic ground. Instead, he saw his chance when his scouts reported that although Washington had Pyles and Wistars Fords covered, he seemed to have forgotten about Jeffries Ford, just eight miles north of his position.

Because Washington had neglected to fully research the terrain, he left his right flank exposed. It was an oversight that was to cost him the battle, and Philadelphia.

The Battle of Brandywine, fought on September 11, 1777, was another 9/11 in our country's history. Like the brilliant strategist he was, Howe split his army into two divisions, one under Baron Wilhelm Knyphausen, the other under Charles Cornwallis. While Knyphausen faced Wayne at Chadds Ford, seemingly falling right into Washington's trap, Cornwallis and Howe snuck over to Jeffries Ford, where they staged a surprise attack on Washington's open right flank. By the time the Patriots knew what had happened, both Knyphausen's and Cornwallis's troops had converged upon them from all sides in a humiliating, costly checkmate.

True to form, however, Mad Anthony Wayne made the redcoats work for their victory. Galloping back and forth across the bloody field, he brandished his saber wildly in the air, exhorting his men to fight to the finish. The worse things looked, the more crazed Wayne became. If they wanted him off that field, by God, they'd have to carry him off!

Wayne obviously was not one to subscribe to that important bit of old Indian wisdom: "When riding a dead horse, dismount." And by the looks of it, he hasn't changed. The phantom Continental officer they say is his ghost rides his dead horse still, haunted by the defeat at Brandywine and somehow spoiling for a second chance. Why else would he cross and recross Chadds Ford, as if trying to figure out what went wrong, or keep galloping up US 1, the site of the old battlefield, as if he's trying to rouse his men for one more go?

But this isn't the only place Mad Anthony's ghost has been seen. There's another, even more famous story, concerning his burial and its bizarre aftermath.

Wayne went on to distinguish himself in the Revolutionary War. His most famous moments were the Battle of Monmouth, where he held out despite overwhelming odds and abandonment by General Charles Lee until Washington sent in reinforcements, and his victory at Stony Point in 1779, when his light infantry overcame British fortifications at the strategic Cliffside redoubt on the Hudson River and boosted the morale of the sorely besieged Continental Army.

After the war, Wayne served in the state legislature and in the U.S. Congress as a representative of Georgia. When the Northwest Indian War began, President Washington recalled his old cohort from civilian life to command a newly formed military force called the Legion of the United States. At Legionville, Wayne established what became the first basic training facility for regular U.S. army recruits.

In 1794 Wayne won a decisive victory against the Indian Confederacy at the Battle of Fallen Timbers, ending the war. The name of the battle, incidentally, was particularly ironic—a few weeks before, a tree had fallen on Wayne's tent, rendering him unconscious. Everyone thought he was a goner, but, as usual, Mad Anthony literally rose to the occasion, climbing out of bed the next day to resume the march to victory.

Two years later, however, Wayne was forced to surrender at last. In 1796, while en route home from fighting Indians in Michigan, he contracted a fatal case of gout and died at the age of fifty-one. He was buried at his request in Fort

Presque Isle—now Erie, Pennsylvania—where the modern Wayne Blockhouse stands.

Here's where the story gets interesting. Thirteen years later, in 1809, Wayne's son Isaac went to Erie to dig up the body and bring it home to the family plot in Radnor, Pennsylvania, for reburial.

But the good people of Erie didn't want their famous general to leave, so a compromise was arranged. They'd keep his flesh, and the Wayne family could have the bones. A Dr. James Wallace was called in to perform the gruesome task of boiling the body in a large vat until the bones were separated from the flesh. Then Wayne's flesh and clothing were reburied beneath the blockhouse, while Isaac Wayne put the bones in a coffin on a wagon and began the long journey home. The story has it that Dr. Wallace was so repulsed by his unsavory duties that he threw his instruments into the coffin as well.

Naturally, the road was bumpy, and somewhere along the 385-mile trail that is today U.S. Route 322, some of the bones fell out of the wagon. The remaining bones were buried in the family plot in St. David's Episcopal Church Cemetery in Radnor. But some months later, on New Year's morning, which is the general's birthday, numerous witnesses reported an odd occurrence. The ghost of Mad Anthony was seen on horseback, on the road where his last journey took place, apparently looking for something.

And every year since, on January 1, his ghost, they say, rises from the grave and gallops along Route 322, in hot pursuit of his lost bones.

Chapter 5

The Hessians Are Coming, the Hessians Are Coming

Can an angry Hessian soldier materialize out of a 200-year-old oil portrait and attack an old man? The former caretaker at the General Wayne Inn will tell you: You bet. Can the disembodied head of a 200-year-old Hessian soldier appear on a kitchen cupboard shelf? The General Wayne's maître d' will swear that it did. Even though they fought and died in an eighteenth-century war, a number of Hessian soldiers have apparently decided to call an old battlefield area of Pennsylvania home for the long run.

It was just another night at the General Wayne Inn in Merion, Pennsylvania. The maître d' was walking by a cupboard in the kitchen when he saw the head of a man slowly materialize on a shelf. The man had a black mustache and was staring at him. When the maître d' gasped in horror, the head faded away.

Terrified screams of "I saw a head! I saw a head!" brought other staffers running to the kitchen. The shaken maître d' described the grisly apparition. No, he hadn't been sneaking snifters from the bar. He was absolutely sober, scout's honor.

The story might have ended then and there, as a case of temporary hallucination, except for two things. One, there was a story, of which the maître d' was unaware, that during the American Revolution, patriots ambushed and killed a Hessian soldier in the building. They decapitated their victim and disposed of his body in the basement.

The other detail that could substantiate the maître d's claim was that for over two hundred years, the General Wayne Inn had been the site of so many reports of ghostly activity, particularly concerning Hessian phantoms, that his was just one more to add to the list.

At about the same time, the new bartender had his Hessian experience. He was hurrying down the stairs to the basement to restock the liquor when he practically collided with a man at the bottom of the stairs, dressed in full Hessian uniform. When the bartender backed up in shock, the soldier turned back toward the basement and evaporated into thin air.

The ghost sightings had differing effects on the witnesses. The maître d' chose duty above self-preservation and continued to frequent the kitchen when necessary. The bartender refused to ever set foot in the basement again. When supplies needed replenishing, he'd give a liquor list to someone else to bring it up for him.

Who were these foreign soldiers who were hanging around the General Wayne Inn more than two centuries after their death? And what unfinished business kept them stuck there?

In late 1775, desperately in need of extra military manpower for the conflict with the obstreperous American colonies, Britain went looking for reinforcements among various Continental powers. Negotiations commenced with the petty

German states, among them Hesse-Cassel. It wasn't the most humane of transactions—the soldiers were purchased like heads of cattle, with terms like "every soldier killed shall be paid for at the rate of the levy money . . . three wounded shall be reckoned as one killed" and other cold-blooded stipulations. In such a way, the British acquired twelve thousand German troops.

The virtual trafficking in human flesh aroused Europe's ire. Many of the British people were outraged, despite the fact that large majorities in Parliament ratified the treaties, and the colonists were even more incensed by, and more determined to fight, the English propensity for inhumanity. Even Frederick the Great, hardly a man of unscrupulous integrity, was so disgusted, the story goes, that whenever any of these hirelings passed through his territory, he registered his indignation by levying on them the usual toll for cattle, maintaining that they had been sold as such.

The Hessians thus were shipped off to America, smarting from the blow of having been treated no better than slaves. Their anger at this insult to their honor would linger after death, with bizarre consequences, particularly in Pennsylvania, the temporary capital state of the newly formed United States of America, and the scene of major early battles like Valley Forge, Brandywine, Chadds Ford, and others.

The Hessians were mercenaries, hired by men whose language and interests were utterly foreign to them. Even though they didn't give a fig about the cause for which they were fighting, they nonetheless possessed the courage and obedience of good soldiers. They distinguished themselves in battle and survived as best they could. After the war, some returned home, while others settled in America, becoming part of the Pennsylvania German/Dutch culture that has so defined that region.

But some Hessians never found peace on foreign soil. Instead, they were killed and then left to fend for themselves in a shadowy time warp between worlds, where they apparently are still looking for respect and an outlet for their undiminished male energy. And it's said that many of these restless, disgruntled soldiers picked the General Wayne Inn as their way station after death.

The founder of Pennsylvania, William Penn, owned the land on which the inn was built in 1704. It was originally called the Wayside Inn and served as a key stopover for people traveling along the busy Old Lancaster Road that linked Philadelphia to Radnor, Pennsylvania. During the Revolutionary War, the inn housed many troops; George Washington, in fact, plotted strategy there before the fateful winter at Valley Forge. In 1795, the establishment was renamed the General Wayne Inn, after our old friend, General "Mad" Anthony Wayne.

The General Wayne Inn reportedly had at least eight Hessian ghosts who, until the inn was finally closed in 2001 and recently reopened as a synagogue, enjoyed hanging out at the bar. Many pedestrians walking by the General Wayne at night reported seeing an inebriated phantom octet, drinking and cavorting loudly in German. As soon as they realized that they'd been spotted, however, the figures all vanished.

The bar housed some non-Hessian ghosts as well, such as the Neck Blower. Benjamin Johnson, the last owner of the inn, recalled that often, on busy nights when the bar was full, a woman would suddenly jump, as if startled by something. Then she would turn to the man behind her and accuse him of blowing on her neck. The man would deny any such impropriety, whereupon the next woman at the bar would have the same experience, and so on down the line. This happened so often that Johnson came to expect it on busy nights. He suspected the masher was one of the General Wayne's many spectral residents because he'd often been told the story about a certain obnoxious gentleman who was a frequent visitor to the tavern in colonial times and who, as he drank, would grow increasingly bold with the ladies. One night, when he became particularly annoying, he got into a brawl with another man who defended the honor of a girl he'd insulted. The drunk was killed, but Johnson and others were convinced that his ghost was the invisible Neck Blower, still pestering the gals.

Johnson also experienced at least one frustrated ghost in the upstairs room above the former British Barracks Dining Room. He and a staff member were on the first floor when they distinctly heard loud crashes from the room upstairs that sounded like furniture being thrown about. Upon running up to investigate, they came upon a scene of complete disarray. Tables were upended and chairs strewn around, as if there had been a tremendous scuffle. The only trouble was, no one was supposed to be up there, and no one was ever found on that floor. The culprit, it is thought, was the ghost of a Hessian soldier who was locked in the room and died there. Apparently he didn't realize that the door was no longer locked—or that, being a ghost, he could simply walk through the wall and escape at last.

But by far the most amazing, and chilling, story of Hessian hauntings at the General Wayne concerns the Caretaker and the Portrait.

Some years ago, the old janitor who cleaned the building had an experience that cost him his job, and very nearly his sanity. The man—we'll call him Willie—was a longtime employee of the General Wayne Inn and loved his work, with the exception of one duty—cleaning the main dining room. As soon as he entered this room, Willie said, he would be assailed by a feeling of great uneasiness, which he traced to the portrait of a young Hessian soldier hanging on the wall.

There was something sinister about that portrait. Its subject was obviously a man who thought a lot of himself, and very little of others. His expression was arrogant and contemptuous. Handsome, with a curling mustache, he had a mean smirk about him. But it was his eyes that were particularly disturbing. Cold, dark, and glinting, they seemed extraordinarily lifelike. In fact, guests at the inn repeatedly described the portrait as "creepy," as though the Hessian's eyes were following their every move.

The old caretaker always entered the room with trepidation and tried to finish his work there as quickly as possible. He purposely avoided looking at the portrait, but it seemed to make no difference. He could feel those eyes, watching his every move, and, as he said, "The skin on the back of my neck prickled. It was almost as if that Hessian was breathing on me."

One evening, Willie happened to glance at the portrait, and was astonished at how unusually lifelike it seemed. Suddenly the man in the oil painting began to assume a three-dimensional form. The canvas moved and shifted as its subject seemed to emerge from the painting, life-size and obviously enraged. The room, Willie later reported, grew icy cold. He wanted, of course, to run, but he couldn't. His feet were rooted to the floor. Finally, just as the angry Hessian seemed ready to spring out of the portrait, the old man managed to tear himself away from the incredible sight and flee.

Well, that should have been enough to keep Willie out of that room for the rest of his life. But he was happy with his job and didn't want to risk it by shirking any of his duties. So, terrified though he was, he continued to clean the dining room every Monday night—until the autumn evening when the impossible happened.

"I was working fast, to get out of there as quickly as I could, when out of the corner of my eye, I glanced at the painting and couldn't believe what I was seeing," Willie recalled. "The painting was there, but the Hessian was gone! It was the same background, all right, but no person in it—just a black space. I looked around and I saw him. He was standing in the corner, in the same exact uniform that was in the painting. The blue coat, white breeches, gold cap. He was tall, skinny, and mad as hell."

The janitor needed no further prompting. He turned to leave, but the Hessian began striding after him, yelling something in German.

"I didn't understand any German," said Willie, "but I didn't need to. He was yelling, and those black, flashing eyes of his were glowing red. I threw my mop at him and ran, straight out of that inn and as far down the road as I could before I collapsed."

The next morning, owner Benjamin Johnson noticed the mop and bucket still sitting on the dining room floor. He phoned Willie to ask why the items had been left there. The janitor asked if "he" was gone.

"Who?" asked Johnson.

"The Hessian."

"What Hessian?"

"The soldier in the painting."

"Willie, what the hell are you talking about?"

"He came out of the painting," the old caretaker insisted. "I know it sounds crazy but I'm telling you the God's honest truth, Mr. Johnson. He chased me, cussing in German. He was like to kill me! So I up and ran outta there like as if the devil himself was after me!"

"I've got to check this out," said Johnson. "Hold on."

Shaking his head, Johnson went into the dining room. There, on the wall, was the portrait, looking the same as ever, Hessian and all.

Johnson returned to the phone. "Willie? The painting's right there on the wall, and the Hessian's in it as usual. If I were you, I'd get to a doctor. Fast."

"I don't need no doctor," Willie replied. "But you're gonna need another caretaker." And with that the old man quit, and never returned to the General Wayne again.

Part Three

THE WAR
OF 1812

Chapter 6
Fort Erie or
Fort Eerie?

Located on the Canadian side of the Niagara River, Fort Erie was the scene of several violent battles during the War of 1812. In fact, it achieved distinction as the site of the bloodiest battle in Canadian history. Many American, British, and Canadian lives were lost there. No wonder, then, that the old fort is reputed to be haunted by all sorts of ghosts, among them the famous headless and handless ghostly duo—two soldiers who wander the grounds in search of something unknown, but obviously valuable enough to keep them hanging around nearly two hundred years after death.

For years the apparitions of two maimed soldiers—one without his head, the other without his hands—have presented an eerie sight to tourists and staffers alike at Old Fort Erie. The ghostly war vets have been witnessed roaming the grounds at night, looking for something. A head, perhaps? A pair of hands? No one knows, but one thing is for certain: They're an indelible part of the Niagara landscape that saw so much bloodshed in the War of 1812.

Fort Erie was the first fort built in Ontario by the British, in 1764, and was the only stone fort built along the Canadian side of the Niagara River, as part of a network developed after the French and Indian War. The fort got its first taste of action as a supply base for British troops, Loyalist Rangers, and Iroquois warriors during the American Revolution.

During the War of 1812, more men fought at Fort Erie than at any other site on Canadian soil, and it was the site of the only siege in that country. The garrison of Fort Erie fought against American attacks at the Battle of Frenchman's Creek in November 1812. For a couple of years, the fort went back and forth between American and British hands, until the Americans destroyed the coveted stronghold and withdrew to Buffalo, New York.

In 1812 America's leaders considered Canada such an easy conquest that President Thomas Jefferson called it "merely a matter of marching." It seems, however, that he underestimated the region's complexity. Upper Canada proved to be a surprise. Many Loyalist Americans who had migrated to Upper Canada after the Revolutionary War unexpectedly ended up siding with the British during the War of 1812. In Lower Canada, Britain found staunch allies among the English elite, loyal subjects of the Empire, and the French elite, who were counting on the English to help protect the old order from the American evils of Protestantism, Anglicization, republican democracy, and crass capitalism.

Then there was the issue of Britain's obtaining provisions for its troops from the American side—a strange trade that continued throughout the war, despite futile attempts by the U.S. government to stop it.

The main theater at the onset of the war was the West, principally the areas near the Niagara River between Lake Erie and Lake Ontario, and near the St. Lawrence River and Lake Champlain. The United States began operations in the "western frontier" because that was where the idea of war with the British got the most support, from a populace angered that the English had compromised American settlers by selling arms to American Indians.

During the first phase of the war, from 1812 to 1813, inexperienced American commanders got an unwelcome dose of British military expertise. After American Brigadier General William Hull's embarrassing retreat from Canada on July 12, 1812, and the subsequent victory of British Major General Isaac Brock at Fort Detroit, America began to realize that taking Canada would be no piece of cake. Brock went on to the eastern end of Lake Erie but was prevented from invading American territory by a temporary armistice. As soon as the armistice ended, however, the Americans were up and running, attacking across the Niagara River on October 13, 1812. Though the Americans were badly defeated, General Brock was among the casualties, a tough loss for the British.

Because of the difficulties of land communications, control of the Great Lakes and the Saint Lawrence River corridor was vital. On September 10, 1813, the Americans, under the command of Captain Oliver Hazard Perry, gained control of Lake Erie in the Battle of Lake Erie. On May 27, 1813, the Americans captured Fort George, on the northern end of the Niagara River. Later that year, they incurred the wrath of the British and Canadians by setting fire to the village of Newark (now Niagara-on-the-Lake), leaving the surviving inhabitants without shelter, freezing to death in the snow. The British retaliated by capturing Fort Niagara on December 18, 1813, and destroying Buffalo.

By the middle of 1814, their army considerably more disciplined and skilled, the Americans had more victories under their belts. They captured Fort Erie and won the Battle of Chippewa. On July 25, the British launched the Siege of Fort Erie, forcing the Americans to retreat across the Niagara River. In November, however, the Americans retook the fort and put an end to the back-and-forthing by destroying it once and for all.

After the war, the British continued to occupy the ruined fort until 1823. It wasn't until 1937, however, that Fort Erie was restored to the 1812–1814 period, and it officially reopened on July 1, 1939. Today the Niagara Parks Commission owns and operates the fort and surrounding battlefield.

During the restoration, a mass grave of 150 British and three American soldiers was uncovered, and a memorial near the entrance to the grounds marks their remains. At the other end of the property lies an old Native American burial ground. These graves, and the fact that Fort Erie saw some of the bloodiest fighting of the War of 1812, could be the reason it's famed for its hauntings. In fact, there have been so many ghost sightings that the old fort has become a must-see for tourists hoping for a genuine paranormal getaway. The fort is particularly famous for its Halloween ghost tours, which are definitely a cut above the usual contrived "haunted house" spook shows. "We don't need any of that stuff," sniffed Fort Manager Peter Martin. "We have real ghosts."

One of those is the red-jacketed British soldier who walks the grounds and, like most apparitions, vanishes as soon as he's spotted. Dennis McGibney, a maintenance worker at the fort, told of a former groundskeeper who saw the soldier. "As soon as he turned around," said McGibney, "he was gone." The worker never returned to that area alone.

Or there's the mysterious gentleman in the top hat, who has been seen in the Northeast bastion area. According to the many visitors who've glimpsed this strange figure, he appears for a few seconds and then disappears. Jim Hill, superintendent of heritage for the Niagara Parks Commission, pointed out that the headdress of the British Marines uniform from the 1812 period was a top hat.

One of the most famous spirits at Fort Erie is presumed to be the ghost of Captain Kingsley of the 8th Regiment of Foot. The captain died following a fit of violent convulsions, and his deathbed, a main attraction of the officer's quarters, is one of the oldest artifacts at the fort's museum.

No one is allowed near the bed—not even the sole worker assigned to keep the area dusted. "Our staff doesn't touch anything," said Peter Martin. "That's one of the rules. The bed is so old that if you laid on it, it would collapse." And yet, the bedding is often found ruffled, and the captain's pillow has been discovered in all sorts of odd places, including on top of the canopy.

The captain apparently isn't too keen on having his "boudoir" turned into a public gathering place. People taking tours of the fort have reported to guide Darryl Learn that objects seem to have moved by themselves. One couple told Learn that when they tried to stop the door to the room from opening, thinking a breeze had caused it to swing open, they were met with a strong opposing force that came from nowhere.

"The only thing I could think of," Learn remarked, "was that Kingsley was an officer and a gentleman and would expect some privacy."

But by far the most famous ghosts of Fort Erie are the headless American officer and his handless companion. In *Ghosts of War: Restless Spirits of Soldiers,* author Jim Belanger describes his interview with Jim Hill, an authority on the history of the Niagara region, and a reliable witness if ever there was one. Hill has worked at Fort Erie for years and first heard the story about the ghosts from one of the janitors.

"At Fort Erie," said Hill, "there are mainly American ghosts, and a couple of them we think we know a fair bit about. The most prominent legend involves the ghosts of two American soldiers who wander the banks of the Niagara River and the grounds near the old fort on a quest for something. We can only speculate as to what they are seeking. One soldier is headless. The other has no hands. Local folklore said that these figures needed each other because the headless figure couldn't see to help find whatever it was that they were looking for, and if they found what they were looking for, the handless figure couldn't pick it up."

There was one key to the possible identity of the apparitions: the autobiography of Jarvis Hanks, a fourteen-year-old drummer in the 11th U.S. infantry during the War of 1812. In *The Memoirs of Jarvis Hanks,* written sometime between 1831 and 1847, the author described a gruesome incident he witnessed at Fort Erie.

As there were no regular barbers attached to the army, the soldiers used to shave themselves, and each other. One morning several were shaving in succession, near a parapet. Sergeant Waits sat down facing the enemy, and Corporal Reed began to perform the operation of removing the beard from his face, when a cannon ball took the Corporal's right hand, and the Sergeant's head, throwing blood, brains, hair, fragments of flesh and bones, upon a tent near them, and upon the clothing of several spectators of the horrible scene. The razor also disappeared and no vestige of it was ever seen afterwards. The Corporal went to the hospital and had his arm amputated, and a few men rolled up the Sergeant's body in his blanket, carried it out and buried it. Probably less than 20 minutes transpired between the time he sat down to be shaved and the time he was reposing in the home of the soldier's grave.

Jarvis Hanks's memoirs were known to only a select few. "Certainly townspeople had little idea about this particular incident during the siege, a fact that lends much credence to ghosts," wrote Belanger. Nonetheless, there was no hard evidence for Hanks's story until one day in 1987 when workers at Fort Erie made a chilling find.

"About a half a mile from the present British old Fort Erie, on the other end of the defense lines for the Americans, was a cornerstone for a massive fortified camp that the U.S. Army had," recalled Hill. "And at the far end there was a place they called Snake Hill or Towson's Battery. In that area there was a field hospital, and just beyond it was where they were burying the dead. In 1987, in one retired schoolteacher's backyard, they unearthed the remains of twenty-eight American soldiers. One we're sure is Sergeant Wait."

The body was buried fully clothed. Although there was no dog tag or any other identifying information on the remains, there were telltale epaulets. Unlike British sergeants, who wore chevrons or stripes, American sergeants wore epaulets, Hill explained. "The epaulet had a different hook on it than the normal button that a soldier would have on his uniform." This evidence, coupled with the fact that the body had no head, was enough to convince Hill that it indeed belonged to Sergeant Waits.

And what of Corporal Reed? His body was never discovered. And there's the fact that, according to Jarvis, he had lost only one arm, not both hands. Of course, he might have lost the other arm, or hand, sometime later in battle. Or Sergeant Waits's companion might not be Corporal Reed at all, but another unfortunate war casualty he met along his ghostly journeys.

Whoever they are, these apparitions from nearly two centuries past call Fort Erie home and, until they find what they're looking for, undoubtedly will remain the two most intriguing extra attractions at this historic site of victory that came at such a high price.

Chapter 7

The Jilted Lover
of Mongaugon

When Marie McIntosh met a shy young Canadian lieutenant stationed near the Detroit River at the onset of the War of 1812, she made a decision she would live to regret. The night he was to depart for battle, the lieutenant finally got up the courage to ask for Marie's hand in marriage. Although she loved him, the coquettish girl played hard to get. Humiliated, the lieutenant walked out and was killed in battle that night. So began a haunting that should teach any tease a lesson.

For those who have completely forgotten seventh-grade American history, here's a brief recap of the War of 1812. The combatants were the United States and Britain, and included the latter's colonies of Upper Canada (Ontario), Lower Canada (Quebec), Nova Scotia, Newfoundland, and Bermuda. Hostilities lasted from 1812 to 1815 (obviously the peace treaty of 1814 was not very effective). The immediate cause was trade tensions—Great Britain had been at war with France since 1793 and, in an attempt to impede neutral trade with France in response to the Continental Blockade, imposed a series of trade restrictions that the United States contested as illegal under international law. Two other incendiary actions were the conscription of American sailors into the British navy and British military support for the American Indians' defense of their tribal lands against encroaching American settlers.

Mad as hell and not going to take it anymore, the United States declared war on Britain in June 1812. That's where our story begins.

American General William Hull started the ball rolling when he crossed the Detroit River to invade Canada. Although Hull captured Sandwich, after that he inexplicably froze in his tracks and, against all military and common sense, gave the command to withdraw. His soldiers retreated back to Fort Detroit, their tails between their legs. Meanwhile, Canadian General Isaac Brock was emboldened enough by Hull's cowardice to plan an attack on Detroit with the aid of the Indian leader Tecumseh.

A young Canadian lieutenant by the name of Muir (his first name is unknown) was stationed near the Detroit River. He had fallen in love with a beautiful girl named Marie McIntosh, the daughter of a well-to-do Scottish trader. Marie was fond of the lieutenant but found his crippling shyness and rigid adherence to propriety most tiresome. Every week he visited her, and every week he left without declaring the overwhelming feelings that made him tremble before his inamorata.

At the beginning of August 1812, Muir learned that a contingent of British troops and Wyandot warriors in Canada were planning a raid on the small American settlement of Mongaugon, on the other side of the Detroit River, and that he was to lead the British vanguard—an assignment at best dicey, at worst suicidal.

Fully aware of the danger he faced, Muir decided it was now or never. He had to declare his love to Marie. He mounted his horse and sped to the McIntosh estate. Marie was walking alone along a garden path when she saw Muir dismount and stride toward her with an air of purpose that made her heart skip a beat. Never one to pave the way with courtly charm, Muir got right to the point.

"Marie," he said, falling to one knee, "I love you. I have loved you from the moment I first beheld you. Since that glorious day when you graced me with your smiles of welcome and kindness, I have been able to think of no one but you, and to dream of the day when I would ask you for your hand. That day has come. My dearest, will you make me the happiest man on Earth by telling me that you, too, have the same feelings for me?"

One can only imagine the point of agitation that the taciturn young officer must have been at to make such a bold declaration of his deep emotions. It probably took more courage for him to make his ardent proposal than it did to march onto the most hazardous battlefield. It seems incomprehensible that Marie could not have seen this and been touched by it. Instead, however, she appeared unmoved. And not just unmoved—she laughed in her earnest suitor's face!

According to accounts, Marie was not actually scorning Lieutenant Muir—she was simply teasing him, as any respectable young coquette would do. She fully expected him to redouble his efforts to win her, at which point she would relent and reluctantly bestow upon him the prize he had earned by his desperate persistence.

Unfortunately, Marie hadn't counted on her young lover's pride. Having no experience with feminine wiles, and humiliated to his core, Muir turned on his heel and stiffly exited the stage of what was to be not a love story with a happy ending but a genuine tragedy.

Marie waited a few moments. Then she ran down the lane to call Muir back. But he had already galloped off, and all she could see was the flash of his bright uniform in the gathering darkness as he faded off into the distance.

Seized with dread, Marie was even more disquieted when, that evening, her father mentioned a rumor about a coming raid across the Detroit River. Somehow she knew her lieutenant would be involved. Her heart was heavy when she went to bed, and she lay awake for half the night, replaying the events in the garden and tormenting herself with flashbacks of the heartbroken look on Muir's handsome young face. At last she fell asleep, only to be awakened by the sound of footsteps. She opened her eyes and gasped; the figure of a tall man in British military attire stood by her bed looking down at her with a blank expression.

It couldn't be—but it was. Lieutenant Muir. And yet, not the man she remembered from just hours before. This officer was white and lifeless, like a wax figure of the original, and blood streamed from a gaping wound in his forehead. In her 1884 book, *Legends of Le Detroit,* Marie Caroline Wilson Hamlin reported that Muir then made the following little speech, in a hollow, chilling voice:

> "Fear not, Marie. I fell tonight in honorable battle. I was shot through the head. My body lies in a thicket. I beg you, rescue it from the despoiling hand of the savage and from the wild beasts of the forest."

Then he made some encouraging predictions.

> "The Americans will not long exult. Traitors sit around their camp fires and listen to their councils. Our blood has not been shed in vain. The standard

of old England will float again over Detroit. Farewell, and may you be happy."

But the ghost wasn't finished. As if this macabre declaration wasn't bad enough, he then reached out and grabbed Marie's hand, holding it tightly. Marie later reported that the sensation of his fingers was so horribly cold that it cut through her like an icy knife. That was when she screamed and fainted.

Well, it seems hell has no fury like a lieutenant scorned. When Marie came to, she tried desperately to wish the whole awful incident away as just a nightmare. But on her hand was the bruised imprint of her dead visitor's fingers.

Determined to atone for her cruelty, Marie got dressed, mounted her horse, and headed for General Brock's camp. At Fort Malden, she went to a friend of her father's, the Wyandot war chief Walk in the Water, and begged him to escort her across the river to the battlefield. When she told him about the apparition of Lieutenant Muir, Walk in the Water was visibly shaken. Then he and a band of fellow warriors took her by canoe across the river. When they disembarked, Marie went straight to a nearby thicket as though she were following a map. Sure enough, there was the corpse of Lieutenant Muir, with a bullet in his head.

Marie's Wyandot escorts took Muir back to Canada, where he was laid to honorable rest. But the young woman would never again know the lighthearted life she had once enjoyed. Overnight, they say, she aged forty years, into a sad, serious woman who always seemed to be atoning for something. The imprint of Muir's ghostly fingers on her hand supposedly never faded, and for the rest of her life she covered that hand with a black glove.

Marie McIntosh was not the only person who ever saw the ghost of Lieutenant Muir. For years afterward, there were reports of a spectral British officer wandering the woods of Mongaugon. Legend has it that he never misses an annual appearance on August 9, the anniversary of his doomed declaration of love and subsequent death. For her part, Marie McIntosh also made an annual pilgrimage on that sad day, walking from Sandwich to Windsor, Ontario, dressed as a beggar in rags and sandals and collecting money for the poor along the way—a sobering lesson in romantic etiquette that might be summed up thus:

A haunted life is what you'll get
If you try to play the coquette!

Part Four

THE
CIVIL WAR

Chapter 8

The Ghost Rider of Little Round Top

During the Battle of Gettysburg—the bloodiest of the Civil War—it was the famous Battle of Little Round Top that marked the beginning of the Union victory. Lieutenant Colonel Joshua Lawrence Chamberlain went down in history as the valiant "Lion of Little Round Top." But was the ghost of George Washington behind his triumph?

Of all the commanding officers of the Civil War, none was more remarkable than Colonel Joshua Lawrence Chamberlain, leader of the valiant 20th Maine. Chamberlain's legendary stand at Little Round Top during the Battle of Gettysburg marked the turning point of the war and earned him the Congressional Medal of Honor.

What made Chamberlain so unique? It's hard to pick just one attribute. A childhood genius who taught himself Greek so he could attend Massachusetts's Bowdoin College, Chamberlain was reared on his father's philosophy that nothing was impossible with a combination of sheer willpower and positive action. At Bowdoin, the young Chamberlain was initially introverted, a shy stammerer who had difficulty fitting in. But with characteristic determination, he embarked upon a self-improvement regimen to overcome these afflictions and eventually won awards in oratory. Soon Chamberlain was the toast of Bowdoin. When he wasn't horseback riding at breakneck speed or winning prizes in composition, he was teaching himself the bass viol and organ, becoming so accomplished at the latter that he was appointed college chapel organist.

After graduating Bowdoin Phi Beta Kappa in 1852, the twenty-four-year-old Chamberlain received a degree from Bangor Theological Seminary and taught himself Latin, French, German, Hebrew, Spanish, Italian, Arabic, and Syriac in preparation for a career in the ministry overseas. He then earned a master's degree from Bowdoin, where in 1856 the former stutterer was elected professor of rhetoric and oratory.

In 1861, at the outbreak of the Civil War, Chamberlain, then thirty-three, felt a strong desire to serve his country. He wanted to enlist, but the Bowdoin powers that be refused to let him go, on the grounds that he was "too valuable too lose." But when Chamberlain applied for and was granted a leave of absence to study in Europe, he went straight to the recruiting office and, in 1862, entered the war as a lieutenant colonel of the 20th Regiment of Maine Volunteers. Needless to say, the hoodwinked Bowdoin staff was not amused.

This slender, refined, bespectacled professor was hardly the type one would expect to become a brilliant commander and indefatigable war hero. Yet Chamberlain did exactly that—first at Gettysburg, then at Cold Harbor, Petersburg, and Appomattox. He was wounded many times, once so severely, at Petersburg, that the doctors thought him lost. Hearing of the gravity of Chamberlain's condition, General Ulysses S. Grant immediately promoted him to brigadier general.

But the redoubtable Chamberlain survived and his postwar life was equally illustrious. He became governor of Maine and later president of Bowdoin College. He worked tirelessly for veterans and never lost his lust for battle; in 1898, at the age of seventy, the feisty old warrior volunteered for service in the Spanish-American War and was genuinely bewildered and crushed when his request was politely turned down. Chamberlain died on February 24, 1914, proving the doctors right—his old Petersburg war wound finally did him in, at the age of eighty-five. Had he lived, he undoubtedly would have volunteered for active duty in World War I.

Well, there you have everything you never knew you always wanted to know about the incredible Joshua Lawrence Chamberlain. But now let's go back to the Battle of Gettysburg and Little Round Top, to find out precisely what famous action earned Chamberlain the Medal of Honor—and what ghostly spirit may have helped him from behind the scenes.

The dates of July 1 to July 3, 1863, are imprinted in history as the battle that turned the tide of the Civil War. It took place in an obscure little Pennsylvania farming town known as Gettysburg, and by the time it was over, 51,000 men were dead—more casualties in one battle than suffered by Americans in any war, past or present—and the wind had turned from South to North.

When news reached Union headquarters that the Confederates were planning a major invasion of the North at Gettysburg, Colonel Joshua Chamberlain and the 20th Maine set out for Pennsylvania from Maryland. They were exhausted and literally in the dark as they marched through the night with no detailed maps and only a vague idea of where they were headed. In the overpowering blackness, with a sky full of clouds and no moon to light their way, they could scarcely make out anything.

At a certain fork in the road—the symbolism is probably no coincidence—the moon, as the story goes, suddenly burst through the clouds, illuminating a strange figure up ahead. As the figure came closer, the men made out a man on horseback, dressed, quite oddly, not in Union blue or Confederate gray, but in a uniform that looked to be from the Revolutionary War—a bright red coat, blue leggings, and a telltale three-cornered hat. His steed was equally compelling—a magnificent animal that gleamed silver in the moonlight. Galloping down one of the roads, he motioned for the men to follow him.

In his memoirs, Chamberlain never mentioned the figure's inappropriate attire. Instead, he wrote, he merely assumed the rider was a staff officer sent to direct them. Chamberlain remembered the rider announcing in an authoritative voice that General McClellan was in command again and was riding up ahead of them on the road.

Now, it's hard to imagine why this news would have gotten anyone excited. George "Do Nothing" McClellan was one of the worst generals in military history, and Abraham Lincoln's greatest embarrassment. A handsome, dandyish man who talked a great game, McClellan had so impressed Lincoln that the president made him general-in-chief of the Union Army at the onset of the war. But McClellan became notorious for planning meticulously but never making a move—even when victory was clearly his for the taking. Eventually Lincoln was forced to relieve him of his command, with the famously quoted comment, "If General McClellan does not want to use the army, I would like to borrow it for a time."

While McClellan's inability to act was, in the words of Ulysses S. Grant, "one of the great mysteries of the war," he was nonetheless beloved by his troops. They felt he had their well-being at heart. So, as Chamberlain wrote, when this mysterious stranger appeared with his news,

> Men waved their hats, cheered until they were hoarse, and wild with excitement, followed the figure on horseback. Although weary, they marched with miraculous enthusiasm, believing their beloved general had returned to lead them into battle.

This, as history confirms, couldn't have been further from the truth; General George Meade was in charge, and fortunately McClellan was nowhere near Gettysburg. But, not knowing this, the men of the 20th Maine got a shot of much-needed faith and confidence at a time when battle plans were at best murky, and their forces were greatly outnumbered by the enemy.

The morning of July 1, the Confederates attacked Little Round Top, a forested hill rising over the Union's left flank and a highly coveted prize for both sides. With its high vantage point, the hill was a strategic gold mine overlooking the southern Union lines. If the Rebs took it, they could demolish Meade's entire flank and win a crucial victory. So, Union survival depended on a strong defensive left flank on the hill. In a glaring oversight, however, Union command had discounted the importance of Little Round Top, instead positioning the army's left flank at the base of the hill, on a pile of boulders ominously known as Devil's Den.

This was where the fighting at Gettysburg began. It was fierce and bloody, with soldiers trading fire from behind the massive boulders and shooting advancing infantry right and left. Meanwhile, the scope of the danger had finally become evident to Union forces when a Union lookout, suspicious of the surrounding woods, ordered a shell to be fired and noticed a flurry of gleaming bayonets shoot up through the foliage. Were the Rebs preparing to take advantage of the distractions down below and charge up the hill unchallenged?

General Meade was immediately wired, and he ordered back that the hill be defended at once. This dubious honor fell to Brigadier General James Barnes, whose beleaguered position became increasingly unenviable as streams of Rebel infantry charged up the hill from all sides. Enter Joshua Lawrence Chamberlain. "You understand," General Barnes informed him, "that you are to hold this ground at all costs!"

The 386 men of the 20th Maine Regiment were single-handedly holding the crest of Little Round Top and protecting the southernmost tip of the entire Army of the Potomac. They were also quickly running out of ammunition. It seemed only a matter of moments before the resilient 15th Alabama would finally rout them and overtake the hill. This was when Chamberlain decided to give the order that was to become one of the most significant, and legendary, moments of military history. Over the roar of the fuselage, the screams of the wounded, and the infamous, blood-curdling "Rebel Yell," the 20th Maine heard the voice of their leader:

"Fix bayonets and charge!"

For several moments the men froze in shock. The order was nothing short of suicidal. To barrel down the hill, straight into the arms of the superior Confederate forces? Nobody moved, until one lieutenant, heroically obeying his commander, charged down the slope alone. Shamed and emboldened, his comrades followed suit, with Chamberlain leading the way—to victory.

It turned out the Confederates were taken completely unawares. Flustered, they floundered around until the 15th Alabama retreated in fear with the cheering men of the 20th Maine on their heels. The enemy laid down their arms on the spot. Chamberlain and his ragtag volunteer unit had saved Little Round Top.

But was it only the courage of the lone lieutenant, or the heroic resolve of Joshua Lawrence Chamberlain, that inspired the men of the 20th Maine to such bravery? Or was it something else?

After the battle, many men reported seeing the mysterious "Ghost Rider" again, this time at the moment they received the order to "fix bayonets and charge!" According to eyewitness accounts, the figure suddenly appeared, sword raised toward the enemy, as if motioning to the men to follow him into battle. The rousing sight supposedly filled them with the courage they needed to follow Chamberlain's orders.

And it wasn't just the Union soldiers who were affected by the lofty figure. According to eyewitness reports, a number of Confederate troops fired at him because he was dressed in blue, the color of the enemy. However, bullets seemed to have no effect on the mysterious rider in the tricorner hat and antique coattails, who, after his duty was done, vanished and was never seen again.

Who was this strange apparition? Word spread that it was General George Washington himself, come back to make sure that the Union he had so passionately fought to create and preserve would endure.

Although Joshua Chamberlain acknowledged seeing a figure he thought to be a staff officer sent to lead them on the road the night the 20th Maine arrived in Pennsylvania, his autobiography never mentioned supernatural forces at play in the victory at Little Round Top. Much later in life, when the old "Lion of Little Round Top" was asked about the "ghost rider," he admitted that he had heard the stories about the apparition of George Washington and that he was open to the possibility of their veracity. "Who among us," he reflected, "can say that such a thing is impossible? I do believe that we were enveloped by the powers of the other world that day, and who shall say that Washington was not among the number of those who aided the country he founded?"

Whether Chamberlain actually saw the spirit of Washington that fateful day in July of 1863, he did feel, all his life, the unmistakable presence of the spirit world. As he wrote so eloquently in *Bayonet! Forward: My Civil War Reminiscences,*

In great deeds, something abides. On great fields, something stays. Forms change and pass; bodies disappear; but spirits linger, to consecrate ground for the vision-place of souls. And reverent men and women from afar, and generations that know us not and that we know not of, heart-drawn to see where and by whom great things were suffered and done for them, shall come to this deathless field, to ponder and dream; and lo! The shadow of a mighty presence shall wrap them in its bosom, and the power of the vision pass into their souls.

Chapter 9

A Veritable Ghost Town: Four Famous Gettysburg Haunts

From ghostly Union and Confederate soldiers roaming the town and battlefield to a hotel poltergeist, apparitions of children dressed in Civil War–era clothing, and ghosts who still aren't ready for their close-ups, there's a reason Gettysburg is known as the "most haunted place in the United States."

Gettysburg, Pennsylvania, isn't just the most haunted of all Civil War battlefields—it's been referred to as the most haunted place in all of the United States. One psychic who visited the area proclaimed it ridiculously haunted: "There are so many spirits around here that if you could see them, you'd be saying 'Excuse me' every two seconds because you'd always be bumping into one!"

Apparitions of Union and Confederate soldiers have been seen in the railroad station, hotels, the post office, streets, shops—so often, in fact, that they're practically taken for granted. When people take tours of Gettysburg, they expect to see at least one ghost, and come away sorely disappointed if the "haunts" don't accommodate them.

One example of spirit sightings by unsuspecting tourists is the story of Joan, a woman who was recovering from cancer surgery when she and her husband decided to enjoy a long weekend in Gettysburg.

Joan and her husband took the bus tour across the battlefield, walked around the area, and visited the cemetery. As she was exploring the area, Joan kept seeing groups of children and was surprised, it being a school day. "Each time I went somewhere," she recalled, "the children seemed to follow me. I remember making comments about their clothing, which seemed strange.

"When we got to the cemetery, four of these children asked me to take their picture. I took them under the big tree as you enter the cemetery. I took several shots at the battlefield and talked to some of the people working at the stores. They told some very tall tales about the ghosts that haunt the area."

Later that day Joan and her husband went shopping. At one store they saw a man and a young boy in period dress. Now, it's not all that unusual to see people in Civil War attire at Gettysburg, where there are many period tours, as well as reenactors.

"The man and boy walked around," reported Joan, "and then asked to play the pipe. The boy played five tunes perfectly, not missing a note. It stopped my husband and me in our tracks. It was as if we could not move for the true beauty of the music."

When they returned home, Joan had her film developed. But as she flipped through the prints, there was no evidence of the children she had photographed.

"There were no kids! Bright green illuminations came out on the pictures. I felt that I was not in control of my thoughts. I kept looking at the pictures. I can describe what was supposed to be there. These kids and this young man spent time with me. How can this be explained?" Joan asked.

Psychics who are familiar with Joan's story are certain that she had indeed encountered a few of the famous "Gettysburg ghosts" and that her experience with cancer most likely opened her psychic channels. "There is a whole unseen realm outside the 'normal' spectrum of perception which is just as real as what our five senses are able to sense," said one psychic. "Also take into account that time is not what we think either. On a psychic level, past, present, and future run as parallel realities. So while we think we are in present time . . . the track which is the past runs alongside very closely and through a very thin veil. Perceptually it is possible to 'see' all the time tracks simultaneously . . . if one is tuned in to the right channel."

To date, the spirit population of Gettysburg has been benign, if at times rambunctious. Visitors have reported lots of mischievous activity, from slamming doors, noisy whisperings, lights going on and off, and unexplained knockings that wake them up at night to acts of real naughtiness. At the famous Farnsworth House, one ghost likes to perform feats of levitation; tourists and locals alike have witnessed objects rise into the air by themselves and then come crashing to the ground. It's the timeout corner for this pesky poltergeist!

But for the most part, the ghosts of Gettysburg are silently stuck in a time warp, either unwilling or unable to leave the place where more lives were lost than in any other battle of the Civil War—or any war in which America has ever fought. The most haunted areas of this literal ghost town seem to be the Cashtown Inn, the Gettysburg Hotel, the Farnsworth House, and, of course, the infamous Little Round Top.

The Cashtown Inn

Located eight miles west of the center of Gettysburg is the historic Cashtown Inn, which bears the dubious distinction of being the site of the first casualty of the Gettysburg campaign. The Cashtown Inn was ground zero for the Confederate Army during the battle. It served not only as a headquarters but also as a hospital, and the premises saw so much agony, amputation, and death that it's no wonder the inn's current owner, Jack Paladino, and his wife have numerous photos that testify to paranormal activity.

One of the most amazing photographs dates from 1905 and is the first documented instance of a Cashtown Inn apparition caught on camera. He has been identified as George Washington Sando, a Confederate soldier. On June 26, 1863, Sando was wounded when Union soldiers invaded the hotel. Doctors operated on him immediately, but he died on the premises. Forty-two years later, in a photo of the inn and innkeeper, the unmistakable image of Sando appears in the background, dressed in his Rebel uniform. Since then, apparitions have continuously shown up in photos. "We've seen everything from skeletons, orbs, and strange figures to generals smoking cigars," says Paladino.

The Cashtown Inn's basement is particularly rife with spirit life. This was the site of a Civil War field hospital, and psychics exploring the area routinely report classic signs of paranormal presence. In the documentary *Haunted Gettysburg*, ghost hunter Mark Nesbitt felt an unseen hand touch him and his arm immediately went cold. Later, voices burst onto Nesbitt's electronic voice phenomena (EVP) recorder during playback. It was as if the room had come alive with soldiers all trying to talk at once. Visibly shaken, the psychic who accompanied Nesbitt reported seeing "many soldiers, and lots of blood."

The Cashtown Inn is also home to an invisible yet busy resident who enjoys turning lights on and off and locking guests in and out of their rooms. "We know it's a ghost, because no one is close to a light switch or door when it happens," Paladino nonchalantly explains—obviously used to the otherworldly prankster.

The Ghost in the Vault

Rivaling the Cashtown Inn for the Supernatural Phenomena Award is the stately Gettysburg Hotel. Dating from 1797, when James Scott first opened his tavern, the hotel was a center of activity during that fateful summer of 1863. President Lincoln also visited the hotel when he was writing his immortal Gettysburg Address.

The hotel is a favorite stopping place for both tourists, who might visit for a few days, and ghosts, who tend to check in for a more open-ended stay. Many hotel guests and employees have reported seeing a mysterious woman in the ballroom. Her gown, which has numerous petticoats and ruffles, is clearly from the Civil War era. One visitor who saw her commented that she was "quite beautiful," and that she danced around the room, as if to an invisible orchestra, and then vaporized into thin air. Another famous ghostly resident is "Nurse Rachel," a Civil War nurse who has appeared numerous times, apparently still making her rounds.

Perhaps the most impressive of the Gettysburg Hotel ghosts is the "Ghost in the Vault." So many guests and employees, including the hotel's managers, have reported sensing an unseen presence and hearing unexplained noises in the basement vault that a team of paranormal investigators was finally called in to check things out. Immediately upon entering the area, team members reported feeling a "cold spot." At the entrance to the vault, the resident psychic reported that someone dressed in nineteenth-century clothing was trying to talk to her. She asked the spirit's name.

"He's saying something like 'Culbertson' or 'Cuthbertson,'" she said. "It's . . . *Cul*bertson. Yes, *Cul*bertson, he's saying."

Meanwhile, another team member had his EVP recorder going strong. Upon playback, there was a great deal of crackling and other noises. The team gave the tape to technical experts, who cleaned it up and replayed it on digitally enhanced equipment. The result sent chills through everybody, as a muffled voice was clearly heard, repeating the phrase "Johnson . . . is . . . president . . . Johnson . . . is . . . president..." Presumably he wasn't talking about Lyndon Johnson!

The team decided to research town records from the Civil War period. Sure enough, to their delighted amazement, they came upon one James Culbertson, a soldier in Company K, Pennsylvania Reserves. Culbertson survived the war and definitely would have been alive at the time Andrew Johnson succeeded Lincoln in office. In fact, it sounded like he might have gotten stuck in the trauma of Lincoln's death and still hadn't gotten over the shock that "Johnson is president"!

The Farnsworth House Ghosts

Like most of the other hotels in Gettysburg, the Farnsworth House is considered "one of the most haunted inns in America." Built in 1810, the Victorian B&B has another distinction: It was the site where Jennie Wade, the only civilian casualty of the Battle of Gettysburg, was shot to death by a Confederate soldier.

On the morning of July 3, 1863, twenty-year-old Jennie stood in the kitchen of her sister's home baking bread for the Union soldiers. She had just finished reading a passage from the Bible when a sharpshooter's bullet passed through two doors and struck her, entering her back below the shoulder blade and piercing her heart. She died instantly. But her spirit, believers say, still roams the Farnsworth House, and many a guest can attest to the eerie goings-on in the room that bears her name. One of the most compelling concerns a couple—we'll call them Tina and Jim Trent—who spent a truly memorable night in the hotel where "ghosts check in but never check out."

Tina and Jim were having an unsettling experience in the Sara Black room, where the light kept going on and off, black shadows moved back and forth, and footsteps could be heard in the attic above them—even though the attic was locked and off limits to guests. The next day they asked to be moved to another room—any other room—and were switched to the Jennie Wade room.

Tina was giving Jim a back rub when the light by the bed went out. She turned it back on and resumed the back rub. Off went the light again. She turned in on a third time. And a third time it went off. By this time both Tina and Jim were so spooked that they decided to sleep in their clothes, should it be necessary at some point during the night to beat a hasty retreat to more normal accommodations.

Soon they heard noises coming from the bathroom. Jim got up to check and found that the water in the tub had been turned on. He turned it off. Before he made it back to bed the water went on again, this time harder. Bravely, Jim went back into the bathroom and turned the faucet off again. But this time the water refused to stop and instead rushed out with even more force.

"So," recalled Tina, "we are now in the dark, with the water running in the bathroom. As we lay there and discussed whether or not we should leave, the wooden window frame on the inside of the room—not the outside—started banging. My husband got up and walked over to the window. The banging stopped. This happened repeatedly. Each time Jim would come back to bed, the banging would start, and each time he got up and went over to the window, it stopped cold. So now we're in the dark, water running, window banging."

It was definitely time to leave. But as Tina explained, the one reason she didn't run screaming from the Farnsworth House and down the street to another hotel was that she was too scared to move. And besides, where would she have run to? The Cashtown Inn? The Gettysburg Hotel? Or how about the Balliderry Inn, dubbed the "Grand Central Station of the ghost world," where transparent images of Confederate soldiers have materialized in tourists' photographs, peering through windows, and roaming the tennis courts that were unwittingly built over a former Reb burial ground?

The couple were finally able to fall asleep. But in the wee hours of the morning, Tina awoke to her name being called. Only it wasn't her current name—it was a stage name she'd used long before, when she was hoping to become an actress in Los Angeles. She poked Jim. "Stop calling me by that name!" she said. Jim groaned, having been awakened from a deep sleep, and rolled over, staring at his wife. "I didn't say anything," he replied. Tina believed him—her husband was telling the truth.

Apparently Jennie Wade wasn't too keen on having company. The couple checked out the following morning. But there's a postscript. When they returned home, Jim discovered the key to the Jennie Wade room in his pocket. "That's nice," said Tina. "So you brought her back with us?" Sure enough, bizarre things started happening in their home. Can a ghost bi-locate? Since we can't explain them to begin with, why not?

Another creepy Farnsworth House experience was reported by a guest who was on a ghost-hunting expedition and found the truth of that old adage "Be careful what you wish for, because you just might get it."

"I have many stories about ghost sightings, but this is my favorite. I went into the attic of the Farnsworth House in Gettysburg, Pennsylvania. The attic had been occupied by two Confederate soldiers during the battle of Gettysburg, and they both died there. It was a very warm October day and I was sitting in the attic with a ghost hunter and lady friend. We were asking the spirits to show us they were there when the ghost hunter's camera just started flashing by itself and you could feel a bone-chilling cold. We looked at each other and the ghost hunter went to take more random photos, and the camera wouldn't work. We told the spirits that we were not here to hurt or bother them. We simply wanted them to make their presence known, whereupon someone or something moved the bench behind me in the corner and actually touched me on the arm with what felt like one finger. Well, needless to say, I was out of that attic like a bolt of lightning, and down the steps and out the door!

"I had a lot of ghostly encounters that day and all my stories are the same things other guests have told and I had no prior knowledge of these stories."

The Farnsworth House attic isn't the only place in Gettysburg where camera equipment malfunctions. Little Round Top is the most notorious spot for photo shoots gone awry, and the reason may lie in an undead Civil War photographer's legacy.

Still Not Ready for His Close-Up?

If the town of Gettysburg is haunted, the nearby battlefield of Little Round Top—now part of Gettysburg National Military Park—is a veritable hotbed of ghostly activity. Over the years, all manner of strange goings-on have been reported by park visitors, from thick mists that suddenly descend on the area at dusk, long lines of lights flashing in the distance, and the sounds of battle, to actual sightings of Confederate and Union troops. Many visitors have reported seeing a transparent apparition in the uniform of a Union soldier, astride a slow-moving phantom horse that plods cautiously down the side of the hill. Others have overheard ghostly conversations that seem to revolve around a coming battle or spotted the figures of soldiers moving slowly through the fog.

But the paranormal phenomenon for which Little Round top is most famous concerns malfunctioning photographic equipment—and a Confederate ghost who may have good reason to resent photographers.

Time and time again, visitors have reported that their cameras simply stopped working in certain areas of the battlefield, particularly those that experienced very high casualties. In the Valley of Death, for instance, there have been so many accounts of brand-new cameras jamming, film suddenly unable to load, shutters refusing to open, and batteries going dead that coincidence has ceased to be a reasonable explanation. Countless tourists have attested to an accompanying cold sensation as well, and a feeling of not being welcome. Yet as soon as they leave the area, their cameras begin working again and they have no more problems.

Devil's Den, the site of heavy fighting on the second day of the battle, is a particularly ornery area that got its name from its inhospitable terrain of massive boulders and desolate scrub and brush, and from the carnage that took place when Confederate forces stormed the area, only to be massacred by Union sharpshooters hidden behind the monstrous shields of granite.

Inexplicable orbs of light and amorphous swirling forms have appeared on photographs taken at Devil's Den. Visitors also report sounds of hoofbeats mingled with the cries of dying men, and silhouettes darting in and out of the boulders.

One apparition in particular may have a grudge against cameramen. He appears to be a Texas infantryman who resembles the dead Confederate soldier lying next to one of the boulders in a photograph that was staged three days after the battle by the famed photographer Alexander Gardner. The commonly held belief is that the ghost is still protesting this blatant act of disrespect. The apparition never speaks but just motions to people and then vanishes.

Another famous ghost of Devil's Den is much friendlier. Park managers have been asked many times about a raggedly dressed, long-haired young man who appears to tourists who are trying to find the best spot for a picture. He has been heard to say, in a slow Southern drawl, "There's yer shot," or "How about them rocks over there?" He seems real enough, and yet, after the visitor has snapped the photo and turned to thank him, he's not there. Even more astonishingly, tourists have reported his faint image appearing in their photos—even though they never saw him when the picture was taken!

Although the identity of these phantoms has never been definitely determined, who they are is not nearly as important as *that* they are. Such apparitions remain a testament to the indisputable fact that—at Gettysburg, anyway—the dead do walk among the living, challenging us never to forget the terrible sacrifice that took place on "this hallowed ground."

Chapter 10

The Ghosts of the Bloody Lane

The heroic "Fighting Irish" of the 69th Regiment of New York went down in history for their unswerving valor at the notorious Sunken Road on the Antietam battlefield, where so many troops were mowed down on terrain that proved fatal to both sides. These fearless Sons of Erin are among many ghosts said to roam the battlefield still, cheering, whooping, and yelling their Gaelic cry of "Faugh a Balaugh," or "Clear the way!"

Of all the battles of the Civil War, Antietam holds the record for the most casualties in a single day. Although loss of life exceeded 50,000 at Gettysburg, Antietam is considered the bloodiest twenty-four hours of the entire war, with 23,100 wounded, missing, and dead claimed on the date of September 17, 1862. To compound the tragedy, neither side won, making it the most devastating draw in American military history. It was also the worst defeat suffered by Union forces under General George "Do Nothing" McClellan, notorious for dawdling his way through the war and missing key opportunities for easy victory.

In September 1862, the Union Army was in bad shape following a terrible thrashing at Manassas. On the 13th of that month, they moved into an area in Maryland that had been recently vacated by Confederate troops. There they discovered a bundle of cigars wrapped in what turned out to be a gift of sheer providence—a copy of Special Order No.

191, which was General Robert E. Lee's plan for the invasion of the north and obviously had been intended for one of his generals. McClellan instantly realized that he had in his possession the enemy's playbook. How could he lose? "If I cannot whip Bobby Lee," the smug McClellan stated when he was presented with the secret message, "then I will be willing to go home."

True to form, however, McClellan promptly proceeded to sit on his derriere. Convinced that Lee's troops outnumbered his—even though it was actually the opposite, with Union troops outnumbering the dirty, starving, exhausted Rebels by more than thirty-five thousand men—he decided against an immediate pursuit. Instead he waited overnight and then started west to South Mountain, outside the small town of Frederick, Maryland.

There, Lee tried to block McClellan but was hampered when he was forced to split his army and send troops to the aid of Stonewall Jackson, who was busy trying to capture Harper's Ferry. It was a perfect opportunity for McClellan to go for the jugular, but, as usual, he wasted precious time in elaborate planning. By September 15, battle lines had been drawn on either side of Antietam Creek, near Sharpsburg, where Jackson joined Lee following the surrender of Harper's Ferry. The Confederate troops moved into position along a low ridge running north and south of town.

On the morning of September 17, Union General Joseph Hooker's artillery fired the first volley at Jackson's men in the cornfield north of Sharpsburg. Rebel losses were high, along with corn, which, it was later reported, was "cut as closely as could have been done with a knife." Meanwhile, over at the old Sunken Road, which divided two farms, Union troops under General D. H. Hill clashed with Confederates in what was to become known as the terrible Battle of Bloody Lane. The Sunken Road became a rifle pit for two Confederate brigades, which mowed down charge after charge of advancing Union troops from the safety of what was essentially a trench—and, incidentally, marked the beginning of the concept of trench warfare in American military strategy.

The tables were turned, however, when Union soldiers reached a vantage point where they could fire down upon the road's defenders. Now the Sunken Road became a death trap. One survivor later wrote that it was like "shooting animals in a pen." Within minutes the road filled with bodies two and three feet deep. Union troops poured into the fatal trench, kneeling on the bodies of the slain Confederates as they continued to fire at their retreating brothers. The carnage became intoxicating: "A frenzy seized each man," one soldier recalled, "as we used up our ammunition and then tossed aside our empty rifles to pull loaded ones from the hands of the dead."

Of the many valiant fighters at the Bloody Lane, the most famous were the 69th of New York, more commonly known as the Irish Brigade. Composed of Irish immigrants, the unit was commanded by Thomas Meagher, a great activist in the cause of Irish freedom. The Irish Brigade was in a class by itself; the men brought along their own priest, to say mass for them on the Sabbath and before battles, and to hear their confessions after regular bouts of heavy drinking and brawling.

The brigade's brawling spirit was at full force when beleaguered Union troops at Sunken Road saw the welcome emerald banner flying on the horizon, and heard the sound of drums and the Gaelic battle cry of "Faugh a Balaugh!" or "Clear the way!" As the "Fighting 69th" charged, their priest, Father Corby, rode among them offering prayers and taunting the gunfire as he dodged across the field to administer last rites to the fallen.

When the emerald banner fell, Colonel Meagher, in the thick of things alongside his men, ordered it raised again. The order was to be repeated seven times; in total, the 69th lost eight color bearers at Antietam, and one flagstaff actually shattered in a man's hands during the intense fighting. By the end of the day, the courageous Irish Brigade had lost 60 percent of their men and had gone down in history as the greatest heroes of Antietam.

Next to Gettysburg, Antietam is considered the most haunted of the Civil War battlefields. At Burnside Bridge, on the battlefield, park rangers, reenactors, and tourists alike say they've heard a ghostly drum roll that beats out a single cadence and then fades away, and have seen balls of blue light—the telltale orbs attesting to spirit presences?

St. Paul's Episcopal Church in Sharpsburg, which was used as a Confederate hospital during the battle, is also a bastion of the unexplained. Residents near the church, as well as tourists spending the night at nearby hotels, have been unnerved by the sounds of screams and sobs coming from the church at night.

Bloody Lane is perhaps the most haunted spot at Antietam. Here, the site of the worst slaughter, eerie occurrences attest to the presence of ghosts of the 69th, for whom the fighting is apparently not over.

Today, in the pristine surroundings of Sharpsburg and the now serene national park at Antietam, numerous tourists have reported hearing the faint sounds of gunfire and screams of wounded men, and encountering the overwhelming scent of gunpowder and smoke near the Bloody Lane.

The Piper House, the residence at one of the two farms that bordered the Bloody Lane, served as the headquarters of Confederate General James Longstreet during the battle, and its barn was turned into a field hospital. Today it's a bed-and-breakfast where countless guests have reported seeing a misty apparition in the doorway of one of the upstairs bedrooms. So many visitors—at different times and coming from all parts of the country—have witnessed this figure that the inn's owners have been forced, quite reluctantly, to admit that the premises "might" be haunted.

Many visitors to Antietam have seen apparitions of soldiers in Civil War uniforms, moving along slowly and cautiously as if trying to avoid stepping on the corpses that once filled the Sunken Road. One man said he saw a group of men in Confederate uniforms walking down the old road. He assumed they were reenactors—until they suddenly vanished. But by far the most compelling accounts of supernatural activity concern the Irish Brigade. One story is particularly amazing.

Antietam is a favorite spot for school field trips. One day the seventh-graders of the McDonogh Boys' School of Baltimore visited the battlefield for a lesson in living history that turned out to provide much more information than anyone had bargained for.

Their teacher, Mr. O'Brien, had organized a detailed tour of the area, complete with volunteer reenactors and the participation of the local park rangers. As they piled out of the school bus, the boys, all dressed in their blue blazers, were in high excitement as the rangers lined them up and showed them the parade drill and the manual of arms.

It got even more thrilling when the reenactors marched in. They demonstrated the workings of the Civil War musket and acted out scenes of a typical soldier's life. This was followed by lunch, after which the boys were taken on a tour of the battlefield.

The tour ended at Bloody Lane. As dusk approached, the boys, stationed apart from each other at the restored split-rail fence, were told to observe a period of reflection about everything they'd experienced that day. Then, as they boarded the buses, O'Brien gave them an assignment.

"I'd like you to make good use of the time on the trip back," he said. "Please write an essay now about your experience today, and what impressed you the most."

Groaning good-naturedly, the boys clambered onto the bus and into their seats, took out their notebooks, and started writing.

When O'Brien collected the essays, he found that the Bloody Lane was the most memorable area for many of the boys. But not for reasons he expected. Over and over again, the students reported hearing the sound of chanting and Christmas carols. Since the boys had been sequestered from each other at the fence during the "reflection" time and had begun writing their essays as soon as they were settled on the bus, there hadn't been time for them to communicate with each other about their thoughts at the lane, the last stop of the day. Another strange aspect of the essays was the fact that the boys who had been posted along the lane between the Anderson Cannon Monument and the War Department Observation Tower—the exact place along the line commemorating the doomed charge of the Irish Brigade—had the most intense experience with the chanting and caroling.

In class the following day, O'Brien questioned the boys. "Can you tell me more about that singing you heard at the fence?" he asked.

"It sounded like a Christmas carol," said one boy. "Yes!" nodded the others.

"What sort of carol?" O'Brien pressed him. "Can you remember the words?"

"Well, it seemed like 'Deck the Halls,'" the boy replied.

"Yeah," a classmate cut in. "You know, 'Fa-la-la-la-la . . .'"

O'Brien felt his skin prickle. The boys could not have known of the Irish Brigade's Gaelic war cry of "Faugh a Balaugh"—pronounced Fa-a-bah-lah.

Chapter 11
Old Green Eyes

The Battle of Chickamauga was one of the bloodiest of the Civil War, just behind Gettysburg in total casualties. Today the battle-field, which is now Chickamauga-Chattanooga National Military Park, is a haunted haven for ghosts of both human and perhaps nonhuman persuasion. The most famous of the supernatural residents is "Old Green Eyes," who has been roaming the area since the early days when the Native Americans christened Chickamauga Creek the River of Death.

It was a cold, foggy night, Denise Smith recalled. The year was 1980, the place: Chickamauga-Chattanooga National Military Park in Tennessee. Smith had just gotten off work at the Krystal Restaurant in nearby Fort Oglethorpe and decided to take a shortcut home, through the park. She was driving slowly because of the fog and rain, when, in her words, "I saw something big in the road about eye level, and all I could see were these big green eyes. It was so foggy I couldn't see a body. I got closer and it just disappeared."

Smith had just witnessed the apparition of "Old Green Eyes"—a ghostly creature that has been seen since the Civil War—and many say before—on the battlefield at Chickamauga Creek that claimed thirty-five thousand lives in September 1863. Variously described as a tall figure with scraggly hair, a disembodied head that floats out of the darkness, and a half-man, half-beast, all the eyewitness accounts of this persistent phantom have one thing in common: the green eyes that glow with phosphorescent malevolence.

Chickamauga Creek is located near Chattanooga, at the Tennessee-Georgia border. It was originally inhabited by the Cherokee Indians, who named it Chickamauga, or "River of Death." Indeed, untimely demise seemed to dog the heavily wooded area, whose overgrown vines and numerous thickets became an unofficial burial ground over the centuries for Native Americans, Civil War troops, and many others. In 1898, when Chickamauga became a training camp for soldiers en route to the Spanish-American War, disease repeatedly swept through the camp, decimating more American troops than the war. And the legacy of death has continued to this day; Chickamauga-Chattanooga National Military Park has witnessed more than its share of murder and suicides and is a notorious dumping ground for victims of murders all over the region.

Does a curse really seem to haunt Chickamauga? Union troops would have said yes. The Battle of Chickamauga, fought between September 18 and September 20, 1863, was one of the last Confederate victories of the Civil War. For over a year, Federal troops had been trying to push the enemy out of Tennessee and to capture Chattanooga, "the gateway to the Confederacy." With its vital railroad lines and key Rebel war industries, Chattanooga was central to Union victory. Control of the region meant open access to Georgia, and the opportunity to divide the eastern Confederacy.

General William Rosecrans and his Army of the Cumberland had the upper hand over General Braxton Bragg's Army of Tennessee in Chattanooga when Confederate reinforcements under General James Longstreet arrived by train. The

Rebels proceeded to lure Rosecrans's troops out of Chattanooga, whereupon they launched a devastating attack on Union forces along Chickamauga Creek.

The Union might have had a chance if Rosecrans hadn't committed a fatal mistake. He accidentally ordered his men to close a gap in the Union line that didn't exist. As a result, he opened up another hole for the Confederates, who plunged through it, routing the Yanks and forcing the whole Union army to retreat in shambles back to Chattanooga.

Revenge came two months later, at the Battle of Chattanooga. This time, with Rosecrans replaced by General George Henry Thomas, and General Ulysses S. Grant in charge of all the Federal troops between the Appalachians and the Mississippi, Union troops were in far better shape. On November 24, 1863, they took Lookout Mountain. The next day, however, was when things really heated up.

The troops under General Thomas attacked the first line of Confederate trenches below Missionary Ridge. Swarming over the trenches, they waited for orders. Suddenly General Phil Sheridan, who was attacking with Thomas, decided it was a good time for a little bravado. Pulling a flask from his pocket, he waved a toast to the Confederate gunners on the ridge. "Here's to you, boys!" he hollered. The toastees responded with a volley of gunfire that showered Sheridan and his men with dirt.

"That was ungenerous!" Sheridan shouted with gentlemanly indignation. "I'll take your guns for that!"

The Union troops took Sheridan's boast as a battle cry. With wild whoops, they charged up the hill toward the Rebel artillery. "Who the hell ordered those men up that hill?" a worried General Grant asked an officer.

"No one," the officer replied. "They started up without orders. When those fellows get started, all hell can't stop them!"

And indeed "those fellows" descended upon the Confederates like a herd of banshees, screaming "Chickamauga" at the top of their lungs. The Confederate gunners fired and rolled shells with lighted fuses down the slope, but the Federals were undeterred. The terrified Rebels beat a hasty retreat. That day not only was a victory for the Union; it also was a settling of a score. The North's humiliating defeat at Chickamauga had been avenged.

Today, Chickamauga-Chattanooga National Military Park is one of the oldest and largest of our battlefield parks. Tall trees line its tranquil paths, sharing the stately manicured grounds with cannons, monuments, and other reminders of the War Between the States. During the day, millions of visitors enjoy its quiet, pristine beauty. But it's not the kind of place you want to hang around in after the sun goes down—unless you're ready for a bona fide ghost encounter.

Rangers and tourists alike have reported the usual odd phantom noises traditionally associated with battlefields, from men moaning and crying to shouts and screams with no visible presences, the unmistakable sounds of combat, and galloping horses where no horses have ever appeared. There have been reports of flickering lights, or orbs, in the woods, accompanied by black shapes that disappear when the viewer tries to get a closer look. Some of the most frequently witnessed apparitions include a headless horseman and the famous "Lady in White."

The horseman is thought to be the ghost of Lieutenant Colonel Julius Garesche, who served under General Rosecrans and was killed by a cannonball at Chickamauga, a casualty of his commander's misguided order to close that nonexistent gap in the Union line. Brigadier General William Hazen, who directed the shallow, temporary interment of Garesche on a tiny knoll nearby, described Garesche's grisly remains in a letter found in the Annals of the Army of the Cumberland:

> I saw but a headless trunk: an eddy of crimson foam had issued where the head should be. I at once recognized his figure, it lay so naturally, his right hand across his breast. As I approached, dismounted, and bent over him, the contraction of a muscle extended his hand slowly and slightly towards me. Taking hold of it, I found it warm and lifelike . . .

Although Garesche was later buried in Washington, D.C., his decapitated ghost seemingly remains at Chickamauga, where many have reported seeing him galloping through the woods at night.

The "Lady in White" is such a familiar apparition at the park that rangers don't bat an eye anymore when people report seeing her. Dressed in a wedding gown, she roams the grounds as if searching for something or someone. She is thought to be one of the many wives, mothers, or lovers who scoured the battlefield the night the carnage ended, looking for the bodies of their dead.

The story goes that one bereaved girl in particular apparently never gave up the search for her missing beau. For years locals talked of the poor, deranged woman who wandered through the woods, glens, and fields of Chickamauga, a lantern lighting her way at night, in an endless quest for the body of her beloved. When she died, she was buried in her white bridal gown. But apparently she was to know no rest even in death.

Of course, sightings of the spectral Lady in White could be attributed to imagination fueled by local legend. But the remarkable thing about this apparition is that she has been glimpsed so many times by tourists from all over the world who have never heard the tale.

It's Old Green Eyes, however, who holds the title of the park's resident spook extraordinaire. Stories of his sightings began springing up almost as soon as the last shots were fired at Chickamauga. And actually, he seems to have been part of the landscape long before the Civil War, when Native Americans told their tales of a vengeful Indian spirit with flashing green eyes who was said to have haunted the area for generations.

When it comes to ghost stories, you can put a lot down to exaggeration and the power of suggestion. But when a down-to-earth park ranger admits to seeing a ghost, you have to wonder. Edward Tinney, historian and former chief ranger at the park, told this unnerving tale:

"One day in 1976, at about four a.m., I went to check on some battle reenactors who were camping out in the park. I was walking near Glen Kelly Road when I saw a tall figure, over six feet in height, walking toward me. It seemed human, and at the same time it wasn't. It had shaggy, stringy, waist-length black hair, greenish-orange eyes, and pointed teeth that resembled fangs. Feeling extremely threatened by this presence, I crossed to the other side of the road. As he—or it—walked by me, he turned and smiled a devilish sort of grin. At that moment a car came down a straightaway in the road. As soon as its headlights hit the figure, it vanished."

Old Green Eyes apparently can take several forms. Although Tinney saw a humanesque figure, the phantom often manifests as just a head. According to one witness who grew up near the park, in Walker County, Georgia, "The battlefield, a beautiful and somber place in daylight, is haunted by the shadows of the past at night. Those who venture there in the fading twilight are best advised to lock their car doors. The apparition can appear without any fore-warning. This ghostly manifestation of one who died on these grounds so long ago haunts every part of the park. The gleaming green eyes can spring forth from nothingness, and the most peculiar aspect of this ethereal being is that one usually sees only the head. Some have seen the head-less body of the apparition, as he searches for his head in the dark of the night. More than one person has seen this extraordinary event."

One young man, a Civil War buff and amateur military historian, witnessed the disembodied version of Green Eyes. Emphasizing that he was not in any way a believer in the paranormal, this man was visiting Chickamauga-Chattanooga park purely for the military history experience and was heading back to his car after visiting the battlefield when he heard a loud groaning coming from the woods nearby. Assuming that someone was hurt, he ran into the woods. He immediately felt a sense of foreboding. Suddenly an aston-ishing sight appeared in the twilight.

"This floating head with glowing green eyes burst out of the trees," he recalled. "This thing wasn't scary—it was terrifying! I just yelled and ran like hell."

Yes, Old Green Eyes has made a believer out of more than one scoffer. Never again, said our Civil War buff, will he dis-count the many stories of ghosts who haunt the battlefield where thirty-five thousand soldiers perished. Neither will Denise Smith, the young woman who took that memorable shortcut through the park one chilly, misty night.

"I'd always thought the tale of Old Green Eyes was just a myth," Smith said, when interviewed about her creepy experience. "Frankly, I never would have believed it in a million years." But after seeing those disembodied green orbs glowing in the night fog at Chickamauga Park, she's changed her tune. To this day, even though Route 27 runs directly from Fort Oglethorpe through the park, Smith refuses to return to the area, preferring to take the long way home.

Chapter 12
Ghosts of the Siege

Before Sherman's infamous March to the Sea, Vicksburg, Missis-sippi, was one of the first Confederate cities to taste the bitter fruit of ruination at Union hands. During the Siege of Vicksburg, more citizens starved than were killed by the bayonet or gun. The hardships were indescribable, and when at last the Stars and Stripes flew triumphantly over the Vicksburg courthouse, the once-proud bastion of the Confederacy was reduced to ashes. No wonder, then, that Vicksburg has a thriving population of ghosts, who apparently still refuse to surrender.

At Vicksburg's famed McRaven House, a Union officer is said to haunt the corridors, repeating the story of his murder over and over. At the grand antebellum mansion Anchuca, a bed-and-breakfast that was once owned by Joseph Davis, brother of Jefferson Davis, president of the Confederacy, guests share the premises with the ghost of a young woman in Civil War–era dress. Down the block, the Duff Green Mansion is home to a cadre of Rebel ghosts who haunt the second floor. And so it goes. Ever since the "Great Siege," Vicksburg has been a hotbed of paranormal activity.

Vicksburg was a vital stronghold for the South when, in the summer of 1863, General Ulysses S. Grant embarked upon an assault that would eventually bring the once-grand gateway to the Mississippi River to its knees. On Vicksburg's high bluffs overlooking the river stood an arsenal of Confederate artillery units that made Union passage virtually impossible. It was imperative that the Federal forces gain control of the Mississippi to secure a supply line for reinforcements to their troops in the South and, at the same time, slice the Confederate army in half, isolating Louisiana, Texas, and Arkansas from their counterparts east of the river.

President Abraham Lincoln was well aware of Vicksburg's importance. He gave Grant orders to take the Mississippi River, no ifs, ands, or buts. "See what a lot of land these fellows hold," he remarked, "of which Vicksburg is the key. This war can never be won unless that key is in our pocket."

Grant couldn't have agreed with him more. And yet, during the winter of 1862–1863, the scrappy commander of the Union forces repeatedly failed to get his army on dry land for a campaign against Vicksburg. The more unsuccessful Grant was, the more confident the Confederates became in the invincibility of the "Gibraltar of the West." In April 1863, General John C. Pemberton, head of the Army of the Mississippi at Vicksburg, whose orders from Jeff Davis were to hold the Mississippi River open, no ifs, ands, or buts, crowed that "Grant's forces are being withdrawn to Memphis" and immediately shipped a huge supply of troops to Tennessee. On April 16, the *Vicksburg Whig* gleefully reported that the Union's gunboats were "more or less damaged, the men dissatisfied and demoralized. . . . There is no immediate danger here."

That very night, as civilians and officers in the city waltzed at a gala celebration ball, the music was suddenly drowned out by flashes of light and thundering explosions. It seems the citizens of Vicksburg had celebrated a little too soon. Yankee gunboats were running the batteries. Pemberton was wrong. Grant wasn't in Memphis. He had merely been laying low while setting his ducks in a row. The Siege of Vicksburg was about to begin.

Grant's first strategy was a series of brilliantly orches-
trated diversions that lured Pemberton's army out of Vicksburg, allowing Union forces to isolate the city and secure
the river. He then assembled his entire army for a massive
assault on Vicksburg that began on May 22 and ended on
July 4 in a critical victory for the North.

For six grueling weeks, the Confederates and some
three thousand civilians held out in hellish conditions
while waiting in vain for Jefferson Davis to send in General Joseph Johnston with reinforcements. Every day, more
than two hundred Union guns pummeled the city. Supplies dwindled, starvation set in, and people began eating mules, horses, dogs, and a vile bread made of dried
corn and peas. Even skinned rats started appearing in the
butcher shops. By the end of June, Rebel soldiers were
reduced to quarter rations, and scores of them began falling ill, many with scurvy.

Houses were in ruins, fences had been demolished for
firewood, and people were covered with filth and lice. Terrified civilians dug caves into the hillsides to escape the
enemy artillery. A young woman by the name of Dora Miller
chronicled the daily horror in her diary.

> The slow shelling of Vicksburg goes on all the time.
> . . . Non-combatants have been ordered to leave or
> prepare accordingly. Those who are to stay are hav-
> ing caves built. Cave-digging has become a regular
> business; prices range from twenty to fifty dollars,
> according to size of cave. Two diggers worked at ours
> a week and charged thirty dollars. It is well made in
> the hill that slopes just in the rear of the house, and
> well propped with thick posts, as they all are. It has

a shelf, also, for holding a light or water. When we went in this evening and sat down, the earthy, suffocating feeling, as of a living tomb, was dreadful to me. I fear I shall risk death outside rather than melt in that dark furnace. The hills are so honeycombed with caves that the streets look like avenues in a cemetery. . . . Surely, if there are heavenly guardians we need them now.

Finally, on July 4, 1863, Pemberton surrendered. And from that moment until 1945, the people of Vicksburg refused to celebrate Independence Day.

The Duff Green Mansion is located on First East Street in Vicksburg. Built in 1856, the elegant three-story mansion is considered one of the finest examples of Palladian architecture in Mississippi. With its grand staircase, high ceilings, and enormous ballroom and dining room, the stately home immediately became a social center for the city's prewar elite. The owners, businessman Duff Green and his wife, Mary, were famous for their lavish parties, until the Battle of Vicksburg put an end to life as the citizens knew it, and nearly destroyed the Greens' home as well. Cannonballs repeatedly shot through the upper floors, which was why, when the mansion was converted into a military hospital for the wounded on both sides, the Confederate injured got the first floor while the Union soldiers were relegated to the more dangerous third floor.

In the basement, which functioned as an emergency room and operating room, many amputations took place.

Because the mansion was built on a hill, the basement had an aboveground window. As the gruesome story goes, amputated limbs were tossed out of the window, and often the piles of arms and legs rose to hideous heights before they were taken away and buried.

Today the mansion is a beautifully restored bed-and-breakfast. But some guests have complained of an overpowering smell of ether and other unpleasantly medicinal scents. These guests, say the owners, are almost invariably doctors or others in the medical profession. Apparently it takes one to smell one.

Many of the ghost sightings at the Duff Green have something to do with missing limbs. Former owners have reported hearing the sound of footsteps on the second floor—where the Union wounded were also housed—when no one is up there. It's thought that the footsteps belong to soldiers looking for their amputated limbs—although if those limbs happened to be feet or legs, where the footsteps would be coming from is a bit of a mystery.

Guests in the Dixie Room have been known to wake up to the rather unnerving sight of a one-legged Confederate soldier either leaning against the mantel or rocking in a chair. Obviously he was once a patient in the hospital and seems to have decided that the elegantly remodeled quarters suit him just fine.

Another soldier has been seen roaming about. Research indicates that he died in the mansion on the way to the operating room. His bloodstains, they say, are still visible in the main hall of the second floor. Other residents from the invisible plane include Mary Green, who is said to be a cheerful spirit and who announces her presence by way of a cool breeze, and a young spirit thought to be the Greens' daughter, who died in childhood and can be heard scampering about and bouncing a ball.

Anchuca, located just a block away from the Duff Green Mansion, is another ghost hunter's dream. Also converted to a bed-and-breakfast, it dates from 1830 and was built by Vicksburg politician J. W. Mauldin in the splendid if somewhat ostentatious Greek Revival style of the time. Surviving the siege in 1863, the house became a shelter for many who had lost their homes during the war. In 1868, Jefferson Davis's brother, Joseph, bought Anchuca. The mansion is truly part of history; the old president of the Confederacy gave his last public speech to the residents of Vicksburg there, on the balcony.

The name Anchuca is a Choctaw Indian word meaning "happy home." Unfortunately, Anchuca was anything but happy for the Archer family. Wealthy merchant Richard Archer bought the house in 1837 and lived there with his five daughters, the youngest of whom was nicknamed "Archie" because she so resembled her father. Archie was Daddy's girl until she fell in love with a man beneath her station. Her angry father forbade the marriage, and ever afterward, Archie refused to speak to him, taking all of her meals in the parlor, away from where he dined, and even refusing to sit down during dinner to annoy Mr. Archer even further. Instead, she ate standing up, by the fireplace.

Supposedly, Archie died at Anchuca of a broken heart (or was it acute indigestion from all those uncomfortable meals?). But her spirit never left the home where she had known such unhappiness. All of Anchuca's subsequent owners and their family members, along with guests and other visitors, have seen the ghost of a young woman. Her favorite spot seems to be the parlor, where she stands by the mantel in her brown dress, staring into the fireplace.

But the Vicksburg Haunted House Award definitely goes to McRaven House, which was already over one hundred years old when the Civil War began. During the siege, McRaven House was used as a field hospital. Bullets with teeth marks in them have been found there, attesting to the terrible agony the wounded must have suffered.

After the fall of the city, the house became the headquarters of Union commandant Colonel Wilson, whom Grant placed in charge of the Federal troops, and a Captain McPherson, who served as the liaison between the occupying army and the town's residents. One night, McPherson failed to return from his usual rounds. Twenty-four hours later, the story goes, he came back, but in an altered form. Dripping with water, his bloody ghost appeared before his commanding officer to report that he had been murdered by Confederate sympathizers and dumped into the river. Sure enough, when Wilson and his men conducted a search, they discovered McPherson's corpse floating in the Mississippi.

The ghost of Captain McPherson has appeared to numerous visitors and residents of McRaven House. The pattern is always the same. He materializes before the shocked onlooker and reports the story of his murder, just as he did with Captain Wilson nearly 150 years ago. Will his tale ever be told once and for all so he can finally let go of his tormented past and leave the physical plane?

Another famous McRaven phantom is John Bobb, who owned the house during the siege and the subsequent Yankee occupation of Vicksburg. Bobb's fiery temper was well known, and one day, when he caught some drunken Union soldiers trespassing in the garden, he threw a brick at them, knocking a sergeant to the ground. The soldiers left, vowing that they would "get" Bobb. The old man immediately reported the incident to the Federal commander of Vicksburg, who was only mildly sympathetic. Upon returning to his home, Bobb was met by twenty-five vengeful Union soldiers, who dragged him to Stout's Bayou, about one hundred yards from the house, and shot him to death in the back and face—the first recorded act of violence perpetrated by Union troops after the siege.

Well, that was the end of old John Bobb—or was it? The current owner of the property, Leyland French, reported that one day in 1984, soon after he moved in and was restoring one of the rooms, a large object hit him from behind with such force that his glasses shattered. The gash in his head required quite a few stitches. When Leyland related the story to one of the home's previous owners, the man nodded as if he'd heard it all before. "That's just one of the bad boys that comes around once in a while," he remarked. "You'd better get used to it." Was the "bad boy" Bad Bobb, still throwing bricks after 144 years? That's the general consensus.

But Bobb is just one of McRaven's many otherworldly residents. A group of Civil War reenactors who were staying at the house reported that they were treated to a piano recital one evening by a woman who called herself "Miss Annie." That would not have been particularly unusual, except that she'd been dead for over one hundred years. It turned out that they had met the ghost of Annie Murray, a spinster who'd lived in the house until she was forced to sell it and move into a nursing home. Later that night, the reenactors were surprised when one of the lamps came on all by itself. That was creepy enough, but what made it even creepier was that the lamp wasn't plugged in. When they related the story to Leyland French, he merely smiled and said that was just Miss Annie's way of letting them know she was watching them.

At least five more ghosts are said to haunt the McRaven House, earning it the well-deserved title of "Most Haunted House in Mississippi." One is reminded of the last line in humorist Edward Gorey's famous poem "The Uninvited Guest," about a strange visitor who appears one day to a family, never speaks, and proceeds to take up permanent residence in their home,

It's been seventeen years, and to this day,
He shows no intention of going away.

Chapter 13

General Beauregard Is Not at Rest

Of all the hauntings of Civil War battlefields and homes, none is more bizarre than the goings-on at the Beauregard-Keyes house. The address of 1113 Chartres Street, in New Orleans's French Quarter, is a highlight of haunted travel tours. After all, what ghost lover could pass up the chance to see an entire phantom battle played out before their eyes?

Within the walls of the grand old Louisiana residence that was once the home of Confederate General Pierre Beauregard, the Battle of Shiloh is still in progress, and the general walks the floors, bemoaning the greatest defeat of his military career.

The house is also well known as the site of a bloody Mafia massacre, which took place in the garden. From the beautifully manicured hedges, they say, comes the odor of fresh gunpowder and the sound of shots being fired. And there have been many reports of strange shadows and figures darting madly around the garden fountain, as if trying to escape a deadly pursuer.

But it's General Beauregard whose presence is most powerful at 1113 Chartres Street, and whose ghost seems obsessed with returning to the bloody scene of a battle that traumatized him for the rest of his life—and beyond.

General Pierre Gustave Toutant de Beauregard—P. G. T. to his friends—was as aristocratic as his name. The handsome, dignified French Louisianan with the perfectly groomed mustache, impeccable attire, and proud bearing seemed destined for greatness. He was born in 1818 in St. Bernard Parish, New Orleans, and from ages twelve to sixteen attended an elite French school in New York. In 1838 he graduated second in his class at West Point. Twenty-three years later, he was appointed superintendent of that famed military academy just before the outbreak of the Civil War.

A Southerner to his core, Beauregard immediately became a proud member of the Confederacy. He was named commander in charge of the defenses for Charleston, South Carolina, and upon ordering the bombardment of Fort Sumter on April 13, 1861, he effectively became responsible for the opening shots of the Civil War. Beauregard became a celebrity in the South. Three months later, the "Hero of Fort Sumter" went on to win the First Battle of Bull Run in Virginia. After Bull Run, Beauregard helped create the Confederate Battle Flag, which became the most popular symbol of the Confederacy.

Short in stature, Beauregard felt a deep kinship with another famous undersized military leader, Napoleon Bonaparte. So he couldn't have been more pleased when his peers gave him the admiring, if somewhat redundant, nickname of "Little Napoleon." It seemed that, like his idol, the Frenchman of the South would also rise to glorious military heights. But that dream suffered a fatal setback when, in April 1862, Beauregard took command of the Confederate forces during the Battle of Shiloh.

The west bank of the Tennessee River became the site of terrible carnage when 65,000 Union troops and 44,000

Confederates slugged it out during the first major engagement in the Civil War's western theater on April 6 and 7. The fighting was fierce and brutal, the casualties massive. Over 24,000 soldiers were declared dead, wounded or missing by the time the battle ended in Union victory.

Now the North had control of Corinth, Mississippi, a major railroad hub for the Confederacy. The loss was a great blow to the South, but even more so to Beauregard. The Rebels had been winning on the first day, whereupon Beauregard, believing that the enemy was defeated, called off the attack prematurely. Whoops. The next day he was forced to retreat when Major General Ulysses S. Grant received reinforcements and unexpectedly counterattacked. The rest, as they say, is history.

It's said that Beauregard was so demoralized by the events at Shiloh that he took a prolonged sick leave without the permission of his commander in chief, Jefferson Davis. Davis, who had never liked "Little Napoleon" to begin with, ordered him stripped of his military rank but was forced to rescind that order in the face of a shortage of skilled officers. Beauregard went on to win distinction in the battles of Richmond and Petersburg, but the black shadow of Shiloh always hung over him. Three years later, as commander of Confederate forces in the West, he met his Waterloo in North Carolina, where he and General Joseph E. Johnston surrendered to the hated William Tecumseh Sherman in April 1865.

After the war, Beauregard led an interesting life. He became a champion of civil rights and suffrage for the recently freed slaves. He served in the government of Louisiana, wrote numerous books about military strategy and the Civil War, and became president both of the New Orleans,

Jackson, and Mississippi Railroads and of the New Orleans and Carrollton Street Railway, for which he invented a system of cable-powered streetcars. In 1888 Beauregard was elected New Orleans's Commissioner of Public works. The "Hero of Fort Sumter" died in 1893, at the age of seventy-five, and is interred in the tomb of the Army of Tennessee in New Orleans's historic Metairie Cemetery. But by all accounts, you won't find him there.

In 1866 Beauregard and his family moved to an impressive mansion on Chartres Street in the French Quarter that had been built in 1826 for wealthy auctioneer Joseph LeCarpentier. Today the mansion is a historic landmark known as the Beauregard-Keyes House, after Beauregard and another famous resident, author Frances Parkinson Keyes.

Beauregard lived at 1113 Chartres Street only two years, but apparently the old LeCarpentier estate made a great impression on him, and vice versa. In 1893, the year of the general's death, people walking by the house late at night reported hearing "the voice." Someone seemed to be gasping "Shiloh . . . Shiloh" over and over in a raspy chant that sounded as if it were coming from a great distance, as if wafting over from another time and place, or another world altogether. There was a terror in that one word, a sense of horror that was so convincing, those who heard it bolted as fast as they could.

Who else could "the voice" belong to but General P. G. T. Beauregard, the man who throughout his life was haunted by the demons of the battle he needlessly lost?

Suspicions were confirmed when the house's then current residents began seeing a semitransparent apparition late at night in the ballroom. Witnesses described a "shimmering" figure dressed in a Confederate military uniform and bearing a strong resemblance to photographs of General Beauregard. They also reported a sudden icy chill whenever the phantom appeared and a pervasive sense of despair so acute that observers could not remain in the room for more than a few seconds.

Not long after the first sightings of Beauregard's ghost, another even more amazing phenomenon was reported. Late at night, the home's occupants would be awakened by a loud commotion in the ballroom. It sounded like a far-off battle, they said, with the sound of cannons booming and men yelling and screaming. When the hearers went down to investigate, they had the shock of their lives. The ballroom had vanished, and in its place was the enormous apparition of the Battlefield of Shiloh itself. Witnesses reported seeing a misty landscape of trees, a river, and hills that resembled an impressionist painting, with exhausted, bedraggled soldiers from both sides of the battle frozen at silent attention.

But it didn't end there. As the gunfire exploded, the soldiers would be mortally wounded. Limbs flew off, cannon shot tore through bodies. The scene was too gruesome to believe. "Men with mangled limbs and blown-away faces swirl in a confused dance of death," wrote Victor C. Klein in his 1996 book, *New Orleans Ghosts*. "Horses and mules appear and are slaughtered by grapeshot and cannon. The pungent smell of blood and decay permeates the restless atmosphere." Some said Beauregard and his troops first appeared in full Confederate dress, then slowly turned tattered and bloody, as if reliving the course of the doomed fight.

It was, by all accounts, like watching a ghostly movie complete with grisly olfactory side effects. Witnesses would stand there, transfixed, unable to turn away as, to their horror, the scene shifted and the dead men changed into grinning skulls. Then, as soon as the first rays of dawn pierced the night sky, the horrific vision would fade away and the ballroom would assume its normal appearance.

It sounds like the most fantastic of ghost tales, too ridiculous to take seriously. But unless the occupants of the Beauregard-Keyes house were all on acid and all having the same bad trip, the story has to be taken seriously. Because not only have subsequent owners witnessed the Shiloh midnight show—so have visitors to the Beauregard-Keyes House, which was opened to the public when the mansion was made a National Historic Site. And those venturing past the house late at night often insist they can hear the sounds of battle coming from inside the house.

Other supernatural occurrences have been reported at the residence as well. Ghost animals seem to be plentiful. One psychic said he saw the spirit of Frances Keyes's cocker spaniel, Lucky, who died—of a broken heart, they say—only a few days after his mistress passed away. The psychic maintained he had the photos to prove it. Others have seen the ghost of a large white cat, presumed to be one of General Beauregard's pets.

The house also has a haunted antique doll collection that belonged to Mrs. Keyes. When the collection is photographed, say witnesses, ghostly mists often appear, and the dolls move randomly in the pictures.

A Mafia murder in the garden some years back has apparently been imprinted on the terrain. Many have heard gunshots and smelled the pungent odor of gunpowder or seen transparent, shadowy images running around the old cast-iron fountain. And then there's the story of Paul Munni, a world-class chess master who, they say, went insane while living in the Beauregard-Keyes House (actually, who wouldn't?). The story goes that Munni ran naked out of the house to Ursulines Avenue, brandishing a big ax and threatening to kill the first person to cross his path. Fortunately, the police subdued him before he could carry out his heinous intentions.

Though Munni has long since departed, his spirit apparently hasn't. An avid amateur pianist, he may still be tickling the ivories. Passersby have reported hearing the sounds of a ghostly piano late at night, along with a man's screams. Many tourists have inquired as to "who lives in the house and plays the piano?" The answer, of course, is no one. At least no one of the corporeal variety.

But the most impressive supernatural event at the Beauregard-Keyes House is still, hands down, the late-night phantom movie of the Battle of Shiloh. Some say the participants are Beauregard and the actual battlefield ghosts; others have postulated that the entire spectacle is a manifestation of the anguished general's memories, which play over and over again on a surreal screen from the projection booth of his tortured psyche. If this is the case, we can only imagine what sort of demons Pierre Beauregard had to contend with in life, and is still battling.

Chapter 14

Neither Is
Henry Wirz

Henry Wirz was one of the most reviled personages of the Civil War. Untold horrors occurred during his tenure as commander of the notorious Andersonville Prison. But even at his execution for war crimes, Wirz never stopped proclaiming his innocence. And many say his ghost has returned to Andersonville, to continue pleading his case.

Of all the horrors of the Civil War, the one that brings to mind man's inhumanity to man most vividly is Andersonville Prison. Those photos of naked human skeletons and horrific living conditions rival anything seen in images of Auschwitz and Dachau. Also known as Camp Sumter, the Confederate penal complex was so notorious for its brutal treatment of Union POWs that to this day, its very mention sends shudders through anyone with a human heart and soul.

So does another name—Captain Henry Wirz, the prison commander who after the war was arrested for "conspiring to impair the lives of Union prisoners of war." If General Pierre Beauregard was the "hero of Fort Sumter," Henry Wirz was the villain of Camp Sumter. His two-month trial was the media sensation of the day and ended in his being sentenced to death. To the bitter end, the haggard defendant protested his innocence, but to no avail. On November 10, 1865, Henry Wirz was hanged, and later was buried in the Mount Olivet Cemetery in Washington, D.C.

But as many have claimed, that wasn't the end of him. A famous ghost, they say, haunts the Andersonville National Historic Site. He's been seen on the grounds and by the road marker for the park, dressed in Confederate officer's garb, a kepi on his head. Those who have gotten a good look at him before he vanishes say he bears an uncanny resemblance to photos of Commandant Wirz.

Heinrich Hartmann Wirz was born in Zurich, Switzerland, in 1822. No academic slouch, he graduated from college in Zurich and went on to medical school in Paris and the University of Berlin, receiving two doctor of medicine degrees. In 1849, following the failed Revolutions of 1848 in the German states, he emigrated to the United States and settled in Kentucky, where he got married and established a successful medical practice.

When the Civil War broke out, Wirz enlisted as a private in the Louisiana Volunteers of the Confederate States Army. In the Battle of Seven Pines, in May 1862, he was badly wounded and lost the use of his right arm. The army found work for him, though, as a prison guard, first in Alabama, then in Richmond, Virginia. Eventually he was assigned to the staff of General John Winder, the man in charge of Confederate prisoner of war camps. This was the ill-fated turning point for Dr. Wirz.

In November 1863, General Winder was sent to the village of Andersonville in Sumter County, Georgia, to check out a possible location for a prison for captured Union soldiers. It looked like a good place—in the Deep South, easy access to the Southwestern Railroad, plenty of fresh water available. And the village's mere twenty occupants could offer little resistance to building such an unpopular facility in their backyard.

Construction began in January 1864. Slaves from local farms were brought in to fell trees and dig ditches for the 1,000-foot-by-780-foot stockade. Originally intended to house no more than four thousand prisoners, Andersonville was soon in trouble. By late February, Union POWs began arriving, and by early June the prison population had swelled to twenty thousand. By July it was at thirty thousand, and all the conditions for a living—and dying—nightmare were in place.

In a bitter irony, all of the elements that would have made Andersonville a better POW camp than others at the time—fresh water, fresh air, access to the railroad, and food and medical supplies—turned into little more than either miscalculations or pipe dreams. The sixteen-acre site was nothing but barren ground, surrounded by swamps—a perfect breeding ground for mosquitoes. Within the rough-hewn stockade, there was no shelter whatsoever for the prisoners, who were left to dig holes in the ground, into which they crawled to escape the unbearable Georgia summer heat. As the South continued to suffer defeats, food supplies to the Confederacy dwindled, until there was barely enough to feed the Rebels, let alone their Union captives. Within a matter of weeks, all the prisoners at Andersonville had to eat was insect-infested cornbread.

The water supply, which might have been sufficient for four thousand inmates, became polluted under the congested conditions. Dehydrated and starving, the prisoners began dying at the rate of more than one hundred a day from dysentery, scurvy, typhoid, and smallpox. Bodies were piled in the hot sun for days, festering and attracting all sorts of vermin. As for latrines, there was only a long trench, which soon filled with excrement, attracting more vermin and emitting a horrific stench in the hot sun. It's estimated that during Andersonville's fourteen-month existence, thirteen thousand men died—nearly a third of the prison population. The only surprise is that anyone survived. One who did later described his entrance into the stockade.

> As we entered the place, a spectacle met our eyes that almost froze our blood with horror, and made our hearts fail within us. Before us were forms that had once been active and erect, stalwart men, now nothing but mere walking skeletons, covered with filth and vermin. Many of our men, exclaimed with earnestness, "Can this be hell? God protect us!" In the center of the whole was a swamp, occupying about three or four acres of the narrowed limits, and a part of this marshy place had been used by the prisoners as a sink, and excrement covered the ground, the scent arising from which was suffocating. The ground allotted to our ninety was near the edge of this plague-spot, and how we were to live through the warm summer weather in the midst of such fearful surroundings, was more than we cared to think of just then.

Henry Wirz was made commander of Andersonville in March 1864, just a month after it opened. He immediately acquired the reputation of a brutal and sadistic overseer. He stood by, it's said, while prisoners died agonizing deaths, doing nothing to ease their suffering. He allowed an infamous prison gang known as the Raiders to beat, rob, and kill as they saw fit. Eventually the other prisoners captured the Raiders and Wirz agreed to have them tried. Several of them were hanged, and the others beaten to death by the inmates who still had enough strength to avenge themselves.

Debate still goes on as to Wirz's guilt or innocence. Many said he was a monster, but other reports indicate that he tried to be fair and just under impossible conditions. Some years after his execution, when emotions had died down, people began to see his side. He had not created Andersonville. He had no control over the construction, or the food and water shortages. All he could do was try to maintain some semblance of order in what was essentially hell. He was no better or worse than many prison camp commanders, including those on the Union side, who committed brutal acts as well in facilities that were, in some instances, just as bad as Andersonville. Yet, Wirz's supporters point out, no one in charge of these camps was ever charged or brought to trial. By contrast, Wirz was the only man tried, convicted, and executed for war crimes during the Civil War. Henry Wirz, it began to be suspected, was a scapegoat, sacrificed to assuage the North's outrage over Andersonville and turn the mirror away from the many atrocities that were perpetrated in the Union prison camps.

Has Henry Wirz come back to try to restore his reputation? There is little doubt in witnesses' minds that the apparition they've seen patrolling the Anderson National Historic Site is indeed the infamous prison commander. The officer in the tidy gray uniform of the Confederates is, like Wirz, ruggedly handsome, with a short beard and the kepi the commander always wore to cover his head. Sometimes he patrols the grounds, restless and seemingly inconsolable, shaking his head or talking soundlessly but animatedly, as if trying to explain himself. On other occasions he's been sighted simply standing there, by the road or in the stockade area, a mute testament, perhaps, to his innocence.

It's no surprise that Wirz is hardly the only spectral resident of Andersonville. A place of such horrors would be likely to hold the tormented energies of armies of fallen phantoms. Some believe that the site itself is one big apparition that remembers the events that took place and periodically replays them in the form of a ghostly encounter. They also say that the fact that Andersonville is literally charged with the negative energy of suffering and atrocities explains why nothing has ever grown on the ground, with the exception of rough, resistant nut grass.

The sounds of moans, groans, screams, and marching feet have been heard on the prison grounds, along with gunfire exploding after dark. Visitors have reported seeing ghostly soldiers as well, roaming about the stockade. Some locals believe these are the apparitions of the vicious Raiders, who have come back to control the stockade once again and scare away those who dare to set foot on the premises. When the sun goes down, many locals say they can hear a far-off roar, like a great tumult of people speaking all at once. This would bear out the testimony of one Andersonville POW, who wrote, "The noise of thirty thousand men never really subsided. The stockade echoed all day with a clatter and clamor that rose sometimes to a muffled roar."

One eerie sighting occurred in the prison cemetery. A reenactor couple was leaving the cemetery when the wife turned around to see a man on a crutch, standing beside one of the graves. "He was missing a leg," the woman recalled, "and was wearing a Confederate uniform. My husband saw him as well. We thought he was a reenactor, but we knew they were all back at the camp. We got in our car, and when we drove past the spot, we looked in the rearview mirror. No one was there. Whoever the soldier was had vanished."

But not for long. Others have reported seeing the one-legged soldier with the crutch on the cemetery grounds. He stands there silently, by the grave that could be his own. If the onlookers watch long enough, they get to see him do his disappearing act before their very eyes.

No, there's no shortage of shades at this notorious death camp. As paranormal investigator James P. Akin maintained, "I would suggest that Andersonville is one of the most haunted places in the United States."

Chapter 15
The Creepy Contraband of William Clarke Quantrill

Somewhere in Missouri, or maybe Wisconsin, a stash of plundered gold dating from the Civil War lies buried deep in the silent hills. Legend has it that it belonged to the notorious William Clarke Quantrill and his ruthless guerrilla band—the spoils of their savage raid on Lawrence, Kansas, in August 1863. Legend also has it that it's guarded by ghosts, who'll try just about anything to keep treasure hunters from getting their greedy hands on the blood money.

One of the most infamous characters to grace the annals of American and Civil War history is William Clarke Quantrill. The twenty-something butcher boy of the Ozarks was the leader of a brutal gang of guerrilla fighters known as Quantrill's Raiders, who blazed through Missouri and Kansas in an unofficial scorched-earth campaign that terrorized the Union forces and sympathizers and turned cold-blooded murderers into heroes for the Confederacy. As historian James McPherson observed, "Without any ties to the South or to slavery, Quantrill chose the Confederacy apparently because in Missouri this allowed him to attack all symbols of authority. He attracted to his gang some of the most psychopathic killers in American history."

Quantrill wasn't originally a Missourian. He was born in Ohio in 1837, and from his earliest years he displayed an affinity for cruelty. "This bad seed would shoot pigs through the ears just to hear them squeal, nail snakes to trees, and tie cats' tails together for the pure joy of watching them claw each other to death," noted one historian. Such charming qualities would assure Quantrill a permanent place in the immortal echelons of the world's biggest sociopaths. By the time he was twenty-one, he had already fled several states with the law on his heels and was linked to a number of murders and thefts from Ohio to Utah.

In December 1860 Quantrill joined a group of Kansas Free-Staters who planned to free the slaves of a Missourian by the name of Morgan Walker. But Quantrill couldn't have cared less about the Kansans' cause. He just wanted to have a little fun. Volunteering to "scout the area," he instead located Walker, informed him of the plot, and returned with the slave owner to ambush and kill the four Kansas men.

According to Quantrill, there was a method to his madness. A couple years previously, he and his brother had decided to head west to Colorado. On their way out of Kansas, they were attacked by a band of thirty Kansas Red Legs, a vigilante group of Kansas Free-Staters opposed to the extension of slavery in the western territories, who killed Quantrill's brother and shot Quantrill so many times he was left for dead.

A couple days later, an old Indian came upon Quantrill, who miraculously was not quite dead. He took the young man to his camp and nursed him back to health. While his patient was recuperating, the Indian tracked his stolen wagon and team to Lawrence, Kansas, and at the same time found out the names of all thirty men responsible for the atrocity against the Quantrill brothers. They were, it turns out, all respectable citizens.

The names of his assailants, they say, were seared into Quantrill's heart like a branding iron. He vowed that he would not rest until he had his revenge.

In 1861, at the outbreak of the Civil War, Quantrill joined the Confederates and fought at the Battle of Wilson's Creek in Oak Hill, Missouri. But it didn't take long for the bloodthirsty young Reb to become impatient with the Confederates' reluctance to aggressively pursue the Yankees. Not exactly one to bow to authority, Quantrill formed his own proslavery guerrilla band of a dozen brutal bushwhackers and began to make independent assaults upon Union camps, patrols, and settlements. By 1862, Quantrill's Raiders numbered over one hundred, becoming the most powerful and feared bands of Border Ruffians, and included young outlaws such as Frank and Jesse James, the Younger Brothers, and William "Bloody Bill" Anderson, who used the war's facade as an excuse to rob Union mail, ambush federal patrols, attack boats on the Missouri River, and commit other crimes.

In 1863 General Thomas Ewing, the Union commandant of the Kansas-Missouri border district, launched a brutal campaign against the Confederate guerrillas. He began arresting women and other noncombatants suspected of aiding the Border Ruffians, and crowded them into a dilapidated old building in Kansas City. When the building caved in, killing and maiming scores of women, Missourians were incensed. But Ewing wasn't finished. Shortly thereafter, he issued an infamous order stating that all civilians in the western border counties of Missouri were to be rounded up and driven into exile. Any man, woman, or child who refused to leave would be shot on sight. This was the perfect moment for

Quantrill and his Raiders to come to Missouri's aid and settle a few old scores.

Quantrill had not forgotten his torment at the hands of the Kansas Red Legs. First, he drew up a hit list. Then, on the morning of August 21, 1863, he and his guerrilla forces of nearly five hundred bloodthirsty Confederates roared into Lawrence, Kansas. They dragged the men on the list from their homes and executed them, without so much as a mock trial. By the time the Raiders left Lawrence, the town had been torched to the ground, and 150 Red Legs lay dead.

During the course of the devastation, the Raiders engaged in a heavy looting spree. They loaded their horses with bags of gold and silver, only to be forced to bury the contraband when things got dicey after Lawrence and Union forces went after the terrorists. The story goes that Quantrill and a few of his men quietly stashed their horde in a secret spot near Independence, Missouri, intending to retrieve the booty when things simmered down. But alas, greed goeth before a fall. The Yankees killed many of Quantrill's men, and others left. Finally, Quantrill himself was gunned down in Kentucky.

"Quantrill's Hoard" became a legend. After the war, a number of people went searching for it, with no luck. Only Quantrill and his few trusted lieutenants knew where it was, and dead men weren't talking. As the years passed, the story of the buried treasure grew, and so did the interest surrounding it. Gold diggers never gave up combing the area outside of Independence, trying to find the exact location of the riches.

Then the story began circulating, of a phantom force that stood guard over the spot, determined that no one would ever profit from Quantrill's ill-gotten gains. Apparently someone had gotten close to the plunder, only to be confronted by ghosts dressed in "butternut brown" uniforms who blocked their way. Or treasure hunters would be surrounded by sinister bluish-colored ghost lights that suddenly appeared as they drew near and menacingly came toward them. If, after these creepy warnings, the treasure hunter was still determined to start digging, he or she would get a jolt, as if they'd been struck by lightning. That was usually enough of a hint, and the search would be abandoned. One intrepid woman reported that she had found the spot and struck her shovel into the earth, only to be hurled backward and knocked out by a shower of dazzling sparks. The two men who were with her confirmed her story, adding that when they grabbed the woman and dragged her back to the wagon, hundreds of lights shot into the air in some sort of luminous victory dance.

Through the years, the search for Quantrill's booty has spread outside of Missouri and into the eerie area known as Wildcat Mountain, a famed promontory in Wisconsin that is supposedly the site of not just one buried treasure, but quite a few. Up in the majestic hills shrouded in clouds and fog, a ghostly guard known as the Wildcat Mountain Sentinel is said to patrol the area. The story goes that in the late 1890s, word spread that a wagon train loaded with gold was traveling from Billings, Montana, to Chicago. Soon everybody from treasury agents to highway bandits was looking for it. The man in charge of the transport made a detour into Wildcat Mountain, where he waited until nightfall and then buried the gold high in the rocks. Somehow everyone who knew where the gold was buried mysteriously died soon afterward. But in letters to his family, the wagon-train leader left cryptic clues about the treasure. Today, said John

G., a resident who lives near the mountain, a ghost guards the gold—or rather, lures people away from it.

"This sentinel doesn't stand on top of the gold," John explained. "So when people see this ghost, they aren't going to find anything. That's the whole point. He decoys them away! Throws people off the trail, so to speak." The ghost apparently has also been known to throw rocks, and wields a bowie knife. He is, by some accounts, also a shape-shifter; witnesses have seen him on horseback, standing on the rocks with his rifle, and even in the form of a wildcat. "I saw him in full run on Highway 131 one night," reported John. "I followed him from the Hay Valley Road junction down in the town of Stark until he bounded off on Plumb Run Road."

But the Billings gold may have company. Some say that a portion of the loot buried at Wildcat Mountain and guarded by the Sentinel Ghost may be the contraband collected by the Quantrill Raiders and later hidden by Frank James at his Wildcat Mountain hideout.

Of course, this theory has never been proven and most likely never will be. For the moment, anyway, it looks like the gold in them thar hills is thar to stay.

Chapter 16
The Haunted Ozarks

Ask any Civil War reenactors if they've ever seen a battlefield ghost, and they're likely to stare at you like you're crazy—not because you believe in ghosts, but because it's such a natural fact of life to share the premises with their dead predecessors that it just seems like a thoroughly unnecessary question.

The Battle of Wilson's Creek—the second largest battle in the first year of the Civil War—was a bloody clash that ended in a pricey Confederate victory. General Nathaniel Lyon and his troops were camped near Springfield, Missouri, aware that Confederate forces under General Benjamin McCullough were approaching. Both sides were plotting their strategies when, in the early morning hours of August 10, 1861, Lyon and Colonel Franz Sigel launched a surprise attack on the Rebels at Wilson's Creek, about twelve miles southwest of Springfield. The "Battle of Bloody Hill," as it came to be known, ended swiftly in a temporary Confederate retreat, followed by an all-out attack on Federal forces that claimed the life of Lyon and some 1300 other Union troops.

Although the Rebels technically won the Battle of Wilson's Creek (known in the South as the "Battle of Oak Hill"), they sustained nearly the same number of casualties. The victory, however, was what Missouri needed to move from a position of "armed neutral" to full Confederate status. In October 1861, Governor Jackson authorized an Ordinance of Secession, and southwestern Missouri was formally under Confederate control.

Wilson's Creek National Battlefield is a favorite gathering spot for Civil War reenactors. These enthusiastic hobbyists make history come alive for park visitors, with realistic simulations of military drills and camp life. The reenactors are always happy when ghosts from the war about which they are so passionate show up to join them.

One day, while on an early morning march, a group of Union infantry reenactors spotted a figure on horseback some distance away, slowly following their column. He was dressed in the wide-brimmed hat and cavalry uniform of the Civil War, and the Union reenactors naturally assumed that he was a cavalry reenactor from another group. But when they looked back a few minutes later, the man had disappeared.

When the members of the only cavalry unit present at the event heard about the incident, they were surprised, and not a little shaken. None of their members had yet saddled up in those early morning hours. They checked with the rangers and other reenactors, and could find no explanation for the mysterious rider. And years later, the story still ends with a question mark. In the midst of Civil War wannabe troops, was the unknown soldier on horseback the real thing? With no evidence to the contrary, the reenactors believe that he was, indeed, a ghost, perhaps looking for his regiment.

A massive plateau of uplifted limestone encompassing northern Arkansas and central Missouri, the Ozarks became a key strategic location during the Civil War. The name "Ozarks" is a bastardization of the more lyrical French "aux arcs," the appellation early French traders and explorers gave the area. Literally translated, "aux arcs" means "of the bows," and is thought to refer to the beautiful bows made by the native Osage tribesmen. Or, it could refer to the bends or arcs in the winding Arkansas River, the southern boundary marker of the region.

In June 1861, the Ozarks entered the Civil War. In Boonville, Missouri, located on the northern edge of the Ozarks, a portion of the Missouri State Guard clashed with Union General Lyon's troops. The humiliating result became known as the "Boonville Races." The inexperienced Missourians held their own until some loud shells from Union artillery sent them running in all directions as Lyon's seasoned men picked them off one by one.

After this undignified licking, it took but a few weeks for the raw young Missouri Rebs to improve their skills. After Missouri's Governor Claiborne F. Jackson and State Guard commander Major General Sterling Price shipped them down to the southwest corner of the state, where they could train and link up with members of the Arkansas Confederacy, they got the chance to prove themselves at the Battle of Carthage on July 5, nine miles north of where they were stationed. With their hunting rifles slung over their shoulders, the bumpkins from the boonies routed their outnumbered Union adversary, forcing them back to the town of Springfield, where they made plans to hook up with Lyon's advancing army.

At the Kemper Military School in Boonville, Missouri, ghost stories abound. Kemper, which was active from 1844 to 2002, had a long and illustrious history. Perhaps that's why battlefield ghosts feel at home there. One in particular seemed to have enrolled permanently. For many years, cadets reported seeing a phantom in an "old-fashioned" uniform that apparently dated from the Civil War. He always appeared in a certain doorway of the building known as the old Band Barracks, and he seemed to enjoy making a dramatic entrance. As cadets lounged around, talking and relaxing, he would suddenly materialize before them. Eyewitnesses invariably described him as short, with dark hair, a moustache, and bright, dark eyes that seemed to bore into them. On some occasions he seemed like a transparency, at others more solid. As soon as the ghost had their attention, the cadets said, he would raise his arm as if in a salute. Then he would slowly evaporate.

The old academy's grounds are now abandoned, halls dark and empty, windows boarded up. No one knows if the Kemper Ghost is still there; chances are, since he obviously thrived on an audience, he's moved on to another stage. As to his identity, it's suspected that he might have been one of the casualties of the Boonville Races, who stayed around to regain some sense of dignity after that embarrassing defeat.

On December 7, 1862—another December 7 that "shall live in infamy," at least for the South—Arkansas troops from the Confederate Army of the Trans-Mississippi District, under Major General Thomas Hindman, met the Kansas Division of the Army of the Frontier, led by General James Blunt, in a head-on collision that would end in an inglorious defeat for the Rebels. Hindman's goal was to stop the advance of Blunt into Arkansas and pave the way for an invasion of Missouri.

In late November 1862, Hindman dispatched 2,000 cavalry under General John S. Marmaduke to pursue Blunt and, at the same time, screen the main Confederate force. But Blunt unexpectedly met Marmaduke with 5,000 men and defeated the Confederates in the daylong Battle of Cane Hill.

On December 3, Hindman and his 11,000 ill-equipped troops moved across the Boston Mountain toward Blunt's division. Hindman planned to have Marmaduke engage Blunt in the south so that he could mount a surprise attack on the enemy's eastern flank. But Blunt had telegraphed the commander of the other division of the Army of the Frontier, General Francis J. Herron, to bring in reinforcements from Springfield that would enable him to set up defensive positions around Cane Hill. Hindman now needed another strategy, so he decided to move north and intercept Herron before he could get to Blunt.

Again, Hindman was thwarted. Herron managed to make a forced march and engage Marmaduke's cavalry south of Fayetteville, Arkansas. Now, faced with Blunt coming at him from the rear, and facing Herron to the North, Hindman made the fatal decision to set up a defensive position atop a line of low hills near Prairie Grove, Arkansas.

On December 7, Herron unleashed a two-hour barrage of artillery on Hindman's right flank. By noon, Hindman's artillery was all but disabled and his troops had retreated into hiding on the reverse slopes. Then, deciding to take advantage of the moment, Herron gave the order to advance on the hill rather than wait for Blunt to arrive. This time, the Union forces were repulsed by Marmaduke and Brigadier General Francis A. Shoup, losing half of their troops within minutes. This carnage took place near the Borden House.

Blunt and his troops arrived on the field just in time to prevent Hindman from launching another attack on Herron's forces. His division attacked the surprised Confederates and drove them back onto the hill.

That night, while Blunt was calling up his reserves, Hindman, out of reserves and ammunition, withdrew his troops under cover of darkness. As the enemy slept on their rifles, the Rebels slipped away, ragged, exhausted and demoralized.

The Prairie Grove Battlefield State Park is one of the most intact Civil War battlefields. Located just outside Prairie Grove, Arkansas, about ten miles west of Fayetteville, the park draws many reenactors, one of whom, Steve Cottrell, had an experience with the supernatural that, for a moment, turned simulated reality into reality itself. As he relates in his book, *Haunted Ozark Battlefields:*

"One cool December night, I stood on the front lawn of the Borden House at Prairie Grove Battlefield State Park. Restless and unable to sleep, I was one of the last reenactors still awake after setting up camp late Friday night preparation for the event that weekend. I had taken a solitary stroll to the hill on which the historic old home still stood overlooking the valley from which Union troops assaulted Confederate positions on December 7, 1862.

"As I silently contemplated the history of the grounds on which I stood, I suddenly became aware of hundreds, perhaps thousands, of voices in the distance. At first I thought that maybe a football game was in progress somewhere in the distance. Then I realized what time it was: between 1:00 and 2:00 a.m. There was no sporting event going on at that time of night, especially such a noisy one in a sparsely populated area. The distant roar of the crowd continued while I paced back and forth. I finally relaxed and accepted the multitude of voices as reality. I remained on that hill for some time, listening to those disembodied souls."

As a further testament to paranormal presences at Prairie Grove, Cottrell printed an eerie photograph of a reenactment, taken by park ranger Don Montgomery. It shows a group of reenactors sitting around a small cannon. When the reenactors got the developed film, they were astonished to see the images of three soldiers barely visible through the gun smoke in the background. The men are dressed in Civil War uniforms, and appear somewhat vaporous. The ghostly trio, says Cottrell, were not members of the reenactment group, and no one can remember them being present when the photo was taken.

From the orbs and disembodied voices said to haunt Missouri's 1849 Kendrick House, which witnessed a Confederate cavalry raid in 1863, to the Rebel soldier who appeared to a woman living in "Ghost Hollow," Arkansas, where a brutal battle took place during the Civil War, many tales continue to be told of the haunted Ozarks and their battlefields where the dead still walk the blood-stained earth.

Part Five

THE ALAMO

Chapter 17
Spirits, Spirits, Spirits
Everywhere

Next to Gettysburg, the Alamo is undoubtedly the most haunted spot in America. There have been so many reports of paranormal activity at this legendary Texas landmark that it's considered virtually de rigueur to see at least one ghost there. In fact, the whole city of San Antonio is reportedly so haunted that one of the historic hotels in the area even offers discounted rates to those brave enough to book the rooms on the top floors, which, the hotel knows for a fact, contain a number of nonpaying guests of the spirit variety.

"I'll never go back to the Alamo again," declared Jorge, a San Antonio native. "It was closing time and the guard was locking up. I looked over to where the case is that displays [James] Bowie's knife and I noticed a man standing there gazing into the display case. I figured he must have been an enthusiastic docent because he was all dressed up in old-fashioned clothing.

"Then I realized I was looking at a ghost. I know it sounds crazy, but I realized I could look right through him."

Jorge isn't the only one who's had a ghost experience at the Alamo. In fact, it's possible that more people have seen or felt spirit presences there than haven't. Another San Antonian reported, "I have been to the Alamo many times and I feel the ghosts. Others have seen the ghosts. A man whose clothes are soaking wet who disappears. A monk in prayer. A crying baby. A young boy peering out a window. A defender in buckskin who walks through walls. A wailing woman."

Everywhere you turn, it seems, there's some otherworldly presence at the old Texas bastion, an undying reminder of the terrible battle that took place there in early 1836 and its equally horrific aftermath.

The Alamo's history, of course, goes back long before the battle that cost over 200 Texans and 1,600 Mexican army troops their lives. Originally built as Mission San Antonio de Valero in the 1700s, in honor of St. Anthony of Padua and Marquis de Valero, the Viceroy of Spain, the site was, from its inception, fraught with misfortune. The Indians, who resented the Spanish missionaries' attempts to convert them, repeatedly attacked the structure. Natural disasters, including a devastating hurricane, either halted construction or forced relocation. In 1739 a smallpox epidemic decimated the population of the fledgling community of San Antonio, which centered on the plaza and mission.

It took decades to complete the church, which collapsed several times due to poor construction. Eventually the mission, which had become a miniature walled city that included homes, a granary, and a hospital, was secularized and finally abandoned. In 1802 Spain, preparing against possible French or American settlement of the Texas frontier, sent a company of soldiers to the old mission at Presidio of Bexar. The arrival of Compania Volante de San Carlos de San Jose y Santiago de Parras del Alamo resulted in the change of the mission name from San Antonio de Valera to the Alamo.

By 1809 resentment of the Spanish dictatorship led to revolutionary rumblings among New Spain's oppressed Mestizos, Creoles, and Indians, who, led by famed martyr Father Miguel Hidalgo e Costilla, declared their independence from Spain in the village of Dolores. By 1811 the insurgency had infected San Antonio de Bexar. On January 21, 1811, retired Spanish Captain Juan Bautista Casas joined the rebels and established his headquarters in the Alamo. The revolution spread to the frontier but within six months was suppressed. Casas and Father Hidalgo were executed as traitors.

For the next ten years, rebellion continued to plague the Louisiana-Texas border. Finally, in 1821, Mexico succeeded in forcing the Spanish out of the Americas and realizing its long-held dream of freedom. In an attempt to improve conditions on the frontier, the new emperor, Vicente Iturbide, sent troops to Villa de Bexar. Under their protection, the population of the Alamo began to flourish, aided by a new influx of Anglo-Americans led by Stephen Austin, who was granted permission to settle into the easternmost regions of Mexico.

Within a year, Austin's original colony of three hundred families had grown to more than eight thousand inhabitants. Austin was given full military authority over the young settlement, which soon grew dissatisfied with the state of political affairs. In 1824 the Mexican Constitution was abolished and the liberal government was supplanted by a military dictatorship under Antonio Lopez de Santa Anna. Anglos began to chafe under the new rulership, which denied them landownership and other rights.

By 1835 the situation had reached critical mass. Santa Anna appointed himself emperor of Mexico, becoming the "Napoleon of the West." The Texans demanded self-government, and

Santa Anna grew more and more imperious and intractable. With supreme arrogance, he proclaimed that the Mexican people were not "advanced" enough to live in a democracy. Finally he decided upon a policy to exterminate North American influence in Mexican Texas.

The result was the Texas Revolution, the center of which was the infamous Battle of the Alamo. Upon hearing that Santa Anna was leading a large force to San Antonio, James Bowie offered to lead volunteers to defend the Alamo. Among the rebels who heeded his call was Davy Crockett, who arrived with twelve determined fighters from Tennessee. But from the outset, the battle was heavily stacked against the rebel defenders, only a few hundred in number, and the Mexican Army's four thousand–plus troops. The Texans fought to the last man, managing to hold the Alamo for thirteen bloody days, from February 23 to March 6, 1836.

When at last the exhausted defenders' supplies gave out, Santa Anna gave the order to kill every last one of them. On March 6 the Mexican army stormed the Alamo compound and the massacre began. The rebels were systematically gunned down, bayoneted, and hacked to death. Only a handful of women and children were spared. Boys as young as twelve were murdered in cold blood. By dawn the following morning, bodies were strewn everywhere. Santa Anna ordered them all—including any who were still alive—burned upon three funeral pyres. Many years later, an old man who had witnessed the horrific spectacle as a child said that the stench of charred flesh was still with him.

As soon as the literal flames died down, the ghost sightings began. The first account of a supernatural presence came just a few days after the fall of the Alamo. Determined that the mission would not become a shrine to its martyrs and their cause, Santa Anna ordered General Juan Jose Andrade to destroy it completely. Andrade passed the buck to a sub-ordinate, Colonel Sanchez, who went with a contingent of men to carry out this final act of desecration.

The men, however, came rushing back without having performed their unsavory duty. They were unable to, they said, because of six *diablos,* or devils, guarding the front of the old mission. As the Mexican troops advanced, the spec-ters lunged at them, screaming and waving flaming sabers.

Dismissing the incident as ridiculous, Andrade went to the Alamo himself to investigate the story. What he found made a believer out of him. He reported that indeed, six ghostly forms protected the mission. Whether the spirits were Mexican or Texican, he didn't know, but he was con-vinced of one thing. "They are protecting the chapel," he insisted. "They died there for a great cause. They will not allow the Alamo to be destroyed."

Paranormal activity has been reported at the Alamo ever since. One of Santa Anna's regimental commanders, General Manuel Fernandez de Castrillon, had opposed the final sav-age assault, warning Santa Anna that it would be a blood-bath. His pleas went unheeded. After the carnage, six men were brought to him alive, after attempting to surrender. Castrillon offered them his protection and petitioned Santa Anna for clemency. Santa Anna responded with the order to immediately execute the men. Castrillon heroically refused, whereupon Santa Anna's staff attacked the prisoners with their sabers, hacking them to death, and almost mortally wounding Castrillon as well.

In the 142 years since that horrific Sunday morning, countless visitors to the Alamo have reported seeing the apparition of a tall, stately Mexican officer, slowly walking through the remaining buildings of the old mission. His hands are clasped behind his back, and he seems to be shaking his head in sorrow. The ghost is presumed to be that of General Castrillon, still grieving over the atrocity he was powerless to prevent.

And every March, a few days after the battle's anniversary, residents of the area surrounding the Alamo report being awakened in the early morning hours by the sound of horses' hooves on the pavement. The rider, they say, is the ghost of James Allen, the last courier to leave the Alamo the evening before the massacre, and now trying to return and report to his commanding officer.

The one defender who turned tail and ran from the battle, earning himself the scornful title of the "Coward of the Alamo," was Louis Moses Rose. His spirit is apparently one of the most impressive pieces of paranormal Alamo evidence. There have been literally dozens of reports of a lone figure, dressed in the period clothing of the Texas rebels, walking slowly and doggedly toward San Antonio from Nacogdoches. When passersby stop him, he repeats the same thing, in a hollow monotone: "I am trying to get back to the Alamo, where I belong." Then he seems to evaporate. The speculation is that this is the guilty soul of Louis Rose, condemned for eternity to return to the battle he ditched.

Then there are the haunted barracks. A member of the Alamo Rangers, whom we'll call Jack, had a chilling experience on the premises during his employment from 1988 to 1991. A sturdy veteran of law enforcement, Jack was hardly the gullible sort. In fact, he prided himself on having both feet planted firmly in reality. When it came to the many ghost stories associated with the Alamo, Jack scoffed.

There was undoubtedly a logical explanation for every one of them, he insisted.

One winter night, after the Alamo closed, Jack was making his rounds, on the lookout for any stray tourists who might still be on the grounds. In the course of his duties, he locked and closed the south end of the long barracks. "I was walking alone through the north end," he reported, "when I began hearing voices. At first I could barely make them out. Then they became louder and louder. Thinking it might be some custodians in the building, I retraced my steps through the south end of the barracks, but there was nobody around. Yet the voices seemed to get louder. I still couldn't make out any words. But on my way out of the building, back at the north end, I did hear a voice, loud and clear, call out, 'It's too late.'"

Jack was unnerved enough to exit the barracks pronto and go straight to his police chief with the story. He knew it sounded crazy, but he also knew what he'd heard. To his surprise and relief, the chief didn't seem the least bit shocked. In fact, he just smiled and nodded.

"He told me that what I'd experienced was pretty normal by Alamo standards," Jack recalled. "It was consistent, he said, with the long list of stories about supernatural occurrences on the grounds. He also said that the long barracks had served as the hospital during the battle, and that men defended the plaza from the roof. That was supposedly where Davy Crockett's famous last stand took place. To this day, I wonder if that voice I heard saying, 'It's too late,' was one of the defenders, seeing the approach of Santa Anna's troops."

Ranger accounts of strange happenings in the barracks are so numerous that they probably would fill a book of their own. Here's another one: Ranger "Al" was on the grave-yard shift—in more ways than one, it turns out—on a cold winter night in 1978. Al was just about to make his routine inspection of the long barracks when he heard the sound of voices coming from inside.

"As soon as I went in, the voices got real quiet," he recalled. "I couldn't hear anything but low mumbling. Then I began hearing words. I made out things like 'No!' 'Stop!' 'Here they come!' 'Fire!' 'He's dead!' It was very creepy, I can tell you. I looked through the whole building, upside down and inside out, but I never found anyone there. I know they were ghost voices, from the thick of the battle."

Hauntings apparently extend to the downtown area of San Antonio as well. At the two historic hotels flanking the Alamo, the Menger and the Emily Morgan, hauntings occur with regularity. At the Menger, guests and staff have frequently witnessed ghosts in the older section of the hotel, as well as in the bar, lobby, and guest rooms. The most famous of these spectral residents is Sallie White, a chambermaid who worked at the hotel over one hundred years ago. In 1876 Sallie was murdered there by her deranged husband, who was convinced she had been unfaithful to him. The Menger's owners paid for her burial expenses, and ever since, there have been numerous sightings of a ghostly chambermaid carrying an armful of towels down the hotel's fourth-floor corridor. When anyone talks to her, she simply walks past them. According to the Menger's assistant manager, Ernesto Malacara, "It is our belief that this woman's spirit was so moved by the hotel's gesture in burying her remains that she keeps coming back, working for no salary to repay us. All kinds of people have seen her, but they tend to give the same description: a woman wearing an old, dark-colored uniform—something that has not been worn here for many years."

At the Emily Morgan, named after a prostitute who supposedly delayed General Santa Anna at the crucial Battle of San Jacinto, six weeks after the Alamo siege, the top floors, which were once a hospital and a morgue, are apparently so haunted that any guest brave enough to stay up there gets a hefty discount. But the owners of both the Menger and the Emily Morgan assure everyone that there's no danger; the ghosts are extremely well behaved and always exhibit a courteous attitude.

"These are benevolent ghosts," says Malacara, "and we ask our staff and guests to react to them in a kind way."

Chapter 18
Ghosts in the
Gift Shop

If you'd like a ghost thrown in with your souvenirs, the Alamo gift shop is the place to be. From the legendary little boy in the upper window who appears every February and then vanishes, to the phantom who walks through the wall and the invisible wailing child in the basement, this part of the Alamo is so haunted that many believe it was built on the site where particularly intense trauma occurred during the famous battle.

People see him again and again. A little boy, peering mournfully out of one of the high interior windows above the Alamo gift shop overlooking the courtyard. The fact that a child would be alone in that deserted area is strange enough, but even more unsettling when you realize that there is no physical way for a little boy to climb that high, and there's nothing—save perhaps a forty-foot ladder—that he could have used to make his ascent.

According to eyewitnesses, the boy appears every year, in February. Though various visitors and workers have seen him throughout the years, the descriptions of him are remarkably alike. He has blond hair and is around twelve years old. As the onlookers crane their necks in amazement, baffled as to how he ever got up there and what he'd be doing there, the boy stares down at them with a heart-wrenching expression on his small, sober face. People report that he's never seen as a complete figure, only from the waist up. He doesn't move about—just sits there, surveying everything and everyone in silent sorrow, like a sad little angel perched somewhere between heaven and earth.

A typical sighting concerns that of two teenage girls who were strolling along the path in the courtyard between the chapel and the barracks when they looked up to see a young boy watching them from one of the west-facing upper windows of the gift shop. They described the child as being "maybe eleven or twelve," his pale little face encircled by golden curls. Although they waved to him, he returned neither their waves nor their smiles.

The strange sight mystified the girls. How could this kid have gotten up in that window, and why would he be sitting there all alone? Later, during one of the Alamo's famed ghost tours, they discovered other stories about the phantom boy in a book about the shrine. They both got goose bumps as they realized that they'd had a bona fide ghost experience.

Could this little boy be one of the children who were evacuated from the Alamo during the siege? Legend has it that he returns every year, in the last week of February—when the battle began—to look for his father, who was one of the slain defenders.

There's another ghost boy at the Alamo, too. He wanders the grounds, and apparently the gift shop area in particular. The following story, recounted by amateur Alamo historian James L. Choron, is simply too convincing to dismiss.

"In the summer of 1990, I took my children, Erich, Megan, and Heather, to see the Alamo. Erich was eight years old at the time, Megan was six, and Heather had just turned four.

"Megan, in particular, seemed to be totally spellbound by everything around her. She was completely silent for the several hours that we were in the Alamo, which is completely out of character for 'Miss Marching through Georgia,' who has never, to date, held still for over five minutes in her entire life. Megan could create more raw havoc in a totally empty room than a Viking raid or Sherman's March to the Sea (where she got the nickname), so I should have suspected something when she showed so much interest in something as 'dull' as history.

"As we were leaving the Alamo, Megan looked behind her and waved, then softly and very somberly said, 'Goodbye, Jamie.' She pronounced it 'Hymie,' as in Spanish, although she knew no Spanish at all. I looked around to see who she was waving to, thinking that she had met some new little friend on the tour. To my surprise, no one was in sight. When I asked her who she was talking to, she said, 'Jamie. There he is, right there.' She pointed to a spot directly in front of the Alamo's doors. No one was there. I told her that I didn't see anyone and that he must have gone back inside. 'No!' she insisted, pointing. 'There he is.' I still didn't see anyone. She then described him to me: a Mexican boy, about fifteen or sixteen years old, wearing cotton pants, a white cotton shirt, sandals, and a tall black hat. She said that he had stood beside her the whole time we were in the Alamo and told her about the battle. 'He said that he was there. He said that he's been here an awfully long time and can't go home. He was sad, but he was glad that he found me to talk to.'

"Now, my daughter does not have an imagination. If she says she saw something, she saw it. I had no doubt that she had seen the Mexican boy, just as I had no doubt, from the way she said he was dressed, that he had been a soldier in Santa Anna's army, and that he had, most likely, died on that long-ago March Sunday morning in 1836. I can't help but wonder how many other little children he has befriended over the years, and if it helps him pass the long days that must hang over him terribly. I have also often wondered why someone so young did not pass on. Is he somehow tied to the spot where he died? Is he somehow 'lost' and trying to go home to some long-gone and forgotten village in Mexico?"

At the Alamo, ghosts appear everywhere. In windows and doorways, on rooftops, wandering around in front of buildings and inside them—you name it, they haunt it. One of their best performances is the walking-through-the-wall act. There was, you remember from the last chapter, that incident involving two phantoms who walked through the wall of the rear chapel. Another similar event took place outside the gift shop. Two tile layers who were working in the gift shop stepped outside on break. In broad daylight they saw a man wearing a "funny-looking western outfit" pass right through a wall near one of the gates. As they stared in disbelief, a gift shop employee raced over to them. "Did you see that?" she said with a gasp. "That weird guy who just walked through the wall?"

"When one person witnesses an apparition, it's often cause for skepticism," noted Alamo ghost hunter Martin Leal. "When several people see it, it's very strong evidence for the presence of ghosts." The Alamo has so much of that evidence that you'll find few people who still don't believe in ghosts after visiting the sacred, restless grounds.

Without doubt, the gift shop is one of the most routinely haunted spots at the Alamo. And the gift shop basement seems to be a particularly popular hangout for the afterlife crowd.

One day, two women who worked in the gift shop were down in the basement, taking inventory, when they encountered "a male and female spirit."

"They weren't solid," said one of the women. "They were fuzzy, hazy. We could make out features here and there. The female looked like a Native American woman. She seemed to be wearing a headdress with feathers. The male seemed to be a soldier. He was short and stocky, and looked like he was leaning on a rifle." The figures stood there, the women said, for about half a minute, then faded away.

This was just one of numerous reports of spirit activity down below. In fact, many of the gift shop's employees refuse to venture into the basement alone. Over the years, staff members have reported eerie sounds and sensations, including a loud sobbing that seems to be coming from inside the walls, and a strong feeling of being watched or followed. There also have been reports of formless shadows moving along the walls, in step with the staff member.

A child's crying has been heard in the gift shop basement as well. One afternoon, two coworkers who were in one of the stockrooms began hearing a faint whimpering. It sounded, said one, like a little child trying to get someone's attention. The women looked at each other, acknowledging that they both had heard the sound, which then promptly became louder, until it intensified into a piercing wail. That was enough to send the women packing. Later a janitor admitted that he, too, had frequently heard the wailing. But, being a staunch realist, he insisted "them ghost stories" were just nonsense. His explanation? "Stray cats!"

Then there was the ranger who was patrolling the grounds one October night when he saw a man come out of the side entrance to the chapel and race toward the gift shop. Assuming it was a vandal, he took off after the man. At the front door of the gift shop, he heard noises inside. He was bewildered—how could anyone have gotten across the courtyard and broken into the locked gift shop in less than a minute? He called for backup, and when his partner arrived, the mystery deepened.

"This is perfectly secure," declared the fellow ranger after inspecting the door. "The lock is intact. Nobody's broken in here. And besides, if they had, wouldn't the alarm have gone off?"

"Maybe so, but how do you explain that?" replied the first ranger, gesturing to the sound of footsteps and loud rustling that was coming from inside the gift shop.

The rangers unlocked the door and nervously ventured inside, their flashlights beaming along the dark walls. As soon as they entered the shop, the noises ceased and the room grew very quiet. While one ranger went around back to inspect the locks, the other heard a noise coming from the basement. Yet when he attempted to open the door leading downstairs, he found that it was locked. Great. Two locked doors, no evidence of a break-in, and somebody was in there. Who—or what—was he dealing with?

The ranger unlocked the door and bravely descended the steps into the basement.

"I was immediately hit by a blast of cold air," he later reported. "It was really creepy. But I continued down the stairs, shining my flashlight around. Suddenly I beamed onto a man at the bottom of the stairs, dressed in buckskin clothing. I figured I'd nabbed the intruder—until I saw that my light was going right through him! He looked up at me, I looked down at him, and poof! He vanished."

At least one gift shop ghost has a mischievous side. Several employees had an experience they still can't explain.

"It was a Saturday, 5:30 p.m., and we were closing up," one of them recalled. "We were all really beat; it had been a very busy day, and we had to work Sunday as well. So none of us wanted to hang around. We straightened up, activated the security system, and left. The next morning, we all arrived early to open up and were greeted by an incredible sight. The gift shop's postcard racks were completely empty, and all the postcards were arranged on the counter in nice, neat piles several feet high!

"Well, we figured the rangers were the culprits. They liked to tease us, after all. But then we realized it just couldn't have been them. They'd have known that the security camera would catch them in the act, and they certainly wouldn't have risked their jobs for a silly practical joke."

The rangers were questioned and denied any part in the strange event. In fact, they said that when they'd made their early-morning inspection of the gift shop, they'd found nothing amiss. The postcards had all been on the racks and everything had looked normal.

To this day, no one has any idea who was responsible for the "postcard caper." But whoever it was never showed up on the security cam. Perhaps there's a playful spirit or two among the restless and tortured spirits who haunt the Alamo. After all, isn't there always one joker in every crowd?

Chapter 19
The Chapel
of Sorrows

The Alamo chapel seems to be a gathering place for many grieving and displaced spirits. This is no wonder, given that it is the most sacred section of the mission, and particularly heinous bloodshed occurred there. A buckskin-clad apparition, a ghostly figure in the chapel window, a sobbing woman, and two men clad in 1800s frontier garb are among the ghostly legion of spirits that have been sighted in and around the chapel, where, they say, the Mother of Sorrows still weeps tears of blood, not only for her crucified son, but also for the martyred defenders of this tormented house of God.

During the final brutal attack on the Alamo, a young woman named Susannah Dickinson witnessed indescribable carnage in the chapel. Susannah, her defender husband, their baby daughter, Angelina, and a few other women and black slaves were huddled inside the structure, which was being bombarded by eighteen-pound cannonballs.

"As the Mexican soldiers rushed in," she recalled, "Jim Bowie killed two of them with his pistols before they ran their sabers through him. Then they shot him so many times through the head that his brains spattered on the wall. My husband rushed in and told me that the Mexicans were inside the walls and, if they spared me, to 'love Angelina.' That was the last time I saw him."

Three unarmed Texans entered the chapel and were shot. Defender Jacob Walker, brother of famed mountain man Joseph Walker, came running in, only to be gunned down by the Mexicans, who then hoisted him up on their bayonets. Then Santa Anna's troops forced the women and children into a corner of the chapel, where they remained until Susannah was taken to Santa Anna. On the way she was shot in the calf, and saw Davy Crockett's body lying between the chapel and the long barracks, his telltale coonskin cap by his side.

Miraculously, Susannah Dickinson was not executed. Instead, she was given a letter from Santa Anna, to be delivered to General Sam Houston. Susannah left the ongoing bloodbath to deliver the message. She did not return to the Alamo until 1881. Then, standing in the dimly lit little room at the rear of the chapel, where she had huddled forty-five years earlier with her baby in her arms, Susannah sobbed as she recalled the horrendous events she could never forget.

The chapel remains a place of sorrows. Tourists and staff alike have often reported the sounds of weeping and wailing, and the faint cries of babies in this room, where women and children were forced to witness such violent bloodshed.

A ranger at the Alamo told the following story. One night, during the winter of 1978, he was in the process of securing the chapel when he heard faint voices and the sound of a woman sobbing. A couple of years later, the same ranger was sitting in the security office when he happened to look out the window. Outside, illuminated by the full moon, were two figures dressed in homespun attire that seemed to be from the Alamo period, coming out of the rear wall of the chapel. "I ran outside after them," he recalled. "I figured they were trespassers. But when I got closer to them I could see right through them! And what's even weirder, although they were talking to each other, they weren't making any noise." The ranger says that when he grew near the men, they stared at him and vanished. Later he remembered that there was no door or other opening at the rear of the chapel. "They were ghosts, all right," he insisted. "Walked right through the wall!"

One tourist in particular recalled that in the 1940s, when he was in the military and stationed in San Antonio, he visited the Alamo on a day pass. As soon as he entered the chapel, he was overcome by a strong sensation of grief. The chapel was the only place on the grounds where he felt such a heavy sense of sadness.

Ten years later, while taking a trip through San Antonio with his two young sons, he decided to show the boys the Alamo. Upon entering the chapel, the man reported experiencing the same rush of melancholy. A few years later, while attending a convention in San Antonio, he and his wife visited the Alamo. Again he went into the chapel, and again he felt the familiar overpowering sensation of grief. This time, however, it was so strong that he felt compelled to leave the room at once. When safely in the courtyard, he burst into tears.

"The Alamo is the only place in the world where I have been so affected," said this man. "Even when I personally experienced deep loss—the death of family or friends—I never felt that kind of sadness and grief."

The Alamo Rangers have had their share of encounters with the supernatural in and around the chapel. One, who steadfastly maintained that he does not believe in the paranormal, saw a man in buckskin clothing in the rear of the chapel, near the northeast corner. He held a long rifle and stood at attention. Others have corroborated the ranger's story, adding that they saw a ghostly soldier in a buckskin shirt, pants, moccasins, and a coonskin cap. Is the cap a giveaway, and is that man Davy Crockett, "King of the Wild Frontier," still on the lookout for the enemy?

On another occasion, while on night duty, this ranger said, he distinctly heard the back door to the chapel slam shut. Since all doors and windows are routinely secured after closing time, the ranger was mystified. Was someone in the chapel without permission? Or was it the air-conditioning unit, making one of its frequent strange noises? Going back inside the chapel, he saw another buckskin-clad figure, leaning against one of the viewing boxes.

"He was a little guy, only about five feet tall," the ranger reported. "His head barely reached above the level of the display case. When I went over to him, I froze on the spot as he literally disappeared before my very eyes." Was the frontier ghost a museum buff who simply enjoyed browsing history exhibits? Or was he simply stuck in his last spot on Earth, looking for the portal to the next world?

Our intrepid ranger had one more ghostly encounter, this time on the grassy knoll in front of the chapel. Glimpsing something out of the corner of his eye, the ranger turned to see a figure inside the chapel window, gazing down at Alamo Plaza. "I was seized by a creepy feeling," he remembered. "What would anybody be doing at that window? Very few people had access to that area."

The ranger kept staring at the figure. It appeared to be misty, almost transparent. Then a tourist came along and engaged the ranger in a brief conversation. They discussed the chapel area, and the tourist asked the ranger if he'd ever seen a face in the window. Before he could reply, the tourist continued, "My friends and I have a photo of a man standing inside the chapel window. You can see through him."

"I know," the ranger replied. "He's up there right now." But when they both looked up at the window, the figure had vanished.

The chapel window is indeed a hot spot for ghosts. Someone or something definitely wants to be noticed, it seems. Late one night, another ranger saw a light in the window. He had turned off the chapel lights, he knew, and no one was supposed to be inside. By the time the ranger had ruled out the possibility of the light being a reflection from a car, or perhaps the exterior lighting, it had disappeared. He went inside the chapel and conducted a thorough inspection, but it was empty, so he returned to his post. Presently the light appeared again. The ranger never discovered an explanation for the occurrence but was convinced that at least one unearthly presence was responsible.

The "Window Ghost" has been sighted by quite a few other staff and visitors. Perhaps he's one of those spirits who just enjoy the limelight, a chance to be noticed at last.

Then there's the "Dripping Ghost." This apparition, which manifests as a murky or transparent image, has often been spotted wearing a full-length western coat, standing near the back entrance to the chapel. He appears to be dripping wet, as though he's been out in the rain. But mysteriously, he's been sighted only on sunny afternoons.

One couple reported seeing a strange-looking man in an old-fashioned western coat around the back of the chapel. It was a particularly hot, humid day, and he was the only person around who wasn't in light summer attire. The couple assumed that perhaps he was a reenactor, and watched him as he stood there in the blazing sun, silently staring straight ahead, not acknowledging anyone around him. Then . . . he vanished. In disbelief, the couple searched around the area, but the weird fellow was nowhere to be seen.

The Dripping Ghost has also appeared in other parts of the Alamo grounds. One ranger on night duty said that while he was making his rounds, he came upon a figure dressed in nineteenth-century period attire, standing silently in the area near the library. The ranger was struck by the fact that although it was a cool evening, the man appeared to be soaking wet. In typical apparition fashion, as soon as the ranger approached him, the man disappeared. Although the ranger made a thorough search of the area, the figure never reappeared.

Yet another ranger saw the ghost near the library. Again, he was wearing a long western coat; again he was drenched; again he was standing there silently, staring into the darkness; again he vanished before the ranger's eyes. Who, wondered eyewitnesses, was this anachronistic figure, and what was he staring at, or looking for? No one knows, and in truth, it probably doesn't matter. He's just another Alamo ghost who, for whatever reason, has some sort of unfinished business at the place that has become one of America's most poignant monuments to the cause of liberty.

Part Six

LITTLE BIGHORN

Chapter 20

The Stone House
and Other Mysteries

There are ghosts on the stairs and in the bedrooms. Strange lights pop up in the darkness. The sound of phantom footsteps sometimes grows so loud that windows rattle. Would you want to spend the night at the Stone House?

At the Stone House, on the grounds of the Little Bighorn Battlefield National Monument, you can, people say, see a ghostly female form descending the stairs late at night. No one has been able to identify her, but she seems to be a permanent resident of the 1894 structure, along with a veritable passel of other supernatural occupants. The Stone House is the most haunted residence at Little Bighorn, a historic site that is teeming with so many undead spirits, one wonders if the battle is, or will ever be, truly over.

The Battle of the Little Bighorn, known as Custer's Last Stand in the history books and the "Battle of the Greasy Grass" to the Native Americans, took place on June 25 and June 26, 1876. The most famous action of the Indian Wars, the engagement ended in a great victory for the Lakota and Northern Cheyenne, under their famous leader, Sitting Bull, over the United States' 7th Cavalry under Lieutenant Colonel George Armstrong Custer.

The battle was the result of friction between the U.S. Cavalry and the Sioux and Cheyenne Indians, who defiantly left their reservations in late 1875 in protest over the whites' blatant intrusions on their sacred lands in the Black Hills. An enormous contingent of warriors gathered in Montana with Sitting Bull to fight for their lands. To force the massive Indian army back to the reservations, the U.S. Army dispatched three columns. The plan was to attack in coordinated fashion. But the headstrong Custer had his own ideas.

On June 25, near the Sioux village about fifteen miles from the Rosebud River, Custer spotted a group of about forty warriors. Ignoring orders to wait, he decided to attack before they could alert the main party. But what Custer didn't know was that the warriors in the village outnumbered his troops three to one.

Dividing his forces in three, Custer sent troops under Captain Frederick Benteen to block the Sioux's escape through the upper valley of the Little Bighorn River. Meanwhile, Major Marcus Reno was ordered to pursue the Indians across the river and charge their village in a coordinated effort with the remaining troops under his command. Reno planned a simultaneous attack on both the northern and southern ends of the Indian encampment but, like Custer, was too impatient to take the time to properly scout out the terrain. He was unpleasantly surprised to discover a maze of bluffs and ravines that would prove a formidable obstacle to his strategy.

Nonetheless, 175 of Reno's men attacked the southern end and tumbled right into a hornet's nest. As the Indians swooped down on them, Reno halted the charge and withdrew into the timber and brush along the river. When that position gave way, they retreated uphill to the bluffs east of the river, the war whoops of the Cheyenne and Sioux ringing in their ears.

At approximately the same time, the Indians saw around 210 of Custer's troops advancing toward the other end of the village. A mighty force of Cheyenne and Hunkpapa Sioux crossed the river and charged into the advancing soldiers, who retreated back to a long, high ridge to the north. Meanwhile, Ogala Sioux under the command of Crazy Horse moved downstream and then doubled back in a huge arc, catching the 7th Cavalry in a deadly pincer move. Custer ordered his men to shoot their horses and line the carcasses up to form a protective wall, but that was the last desperate act of a tragically foolhardy man. In less than an hour, the commander and every one of his men were killed. Instead of masterminding a victory, Custer had engineered the worst American military disaster in history.

After the battle, the Indian warriors stripped the bodies and, in a final act of revenge, mutilated all the uniformed soldiers, believing that the soul of a mutilated body would be forced to walk the earth for eternity and thus could not ascend to heaven. It seems they might have been right— and wrong. Not only do the ghosts of the 7th Cavalry haunt Little Bighorn—so do the Sioux and Cheyenne warriors, most of whom survived the battle.

Workers at the visitor center at the Little Bighorn Battlefield National Monument were amazingly unamazed when, one day a few years back, a tourist came running in, badly shaken. He was, he said, a cab driver from Minneapolis. He'd been driving along Battle Ridge when suddenly he seemed to drive right into another time. All around him, soldiers and warriors were fighting, and the sounds of the battle were deafening. The employees did their best to calm him, assuring him he wasn't crazy. He had simply had his Little Bighorn ghost sighting.

The spirits of Little Bighorn are everywhere. Stories of the sounds of Indian warriors charging on horseback through the cemetery are common. Dozens of visitors have reported icy cold spots that seem to spring up from nowhere. One evening a National Park Service law enforcement officer was alone at Last Stand Hill when the temperature suddenly plummeted, sending a chill all the way through him. At the same time, he began hearing the soft murmuring of voices. He didn't stick around long enough to find out whose they were.

Psychics have had field days at Little Bighorn. One saw "twenty to thirty warriors" charging into battle. They were dressed, she said, in full warrior garb, with all their war paint and fancy headdresses with feathers pointed downward. "They seemed to be latecomers on the battlefield," she noted. The psychic was unaware that toward the end of the Battle of the Little Bighorn, a small group of young braves had entered the fighting, dressed to meet the "Everywhere Spirit." They were all killed and afterward were known as the "Suicide Boys."

Another psychic saw a spirit warrior charge a seasonal employee as he dozed. The warrior counted coup—the custom of touching an enemy in battle with a stick or hand—and then turned and galloped past the visitor center down Cemetery Ridge. The employee woke up, startled. "What was that?" he asked.

Yes, almost everywhere you turn, there's something supernatural happening at Little Bighorn. And one of the most popular ghostly hangouts is, by all accounts, the old

Stone House. The structure was originally built in 1894 for the park's first superintendent, A. N. Grover, whose primary duty when he assumed the position in 1893 was to maintain a fragile peace between local ranchers and Crow Indians who were constantly squabbling over the free-roaming cattle in the area, which had to be constantly herded off the national cemetery.

But cattle weren't the only creatures requiring herding. The Crow called Grover the "Ghost Herder" because he lowered the flag at dusk, which, the tribe believed, allowed the spirits to rise from their graves and walk among the living. At daybreak, the raising of the flag supposedly signaled the hour for them to return to their resting places—until the next sundown.

It seems the Crow might have known what they were talking about. Not only did spirits roam all of Little Bighorn—they also reportedly congregated at the Ghost Herder's own house. The superintendent and his family lived in the second-story apartment. The lower level of the Stone House was used for custodial storage and once served as a holding tank for bodies before burial. The residence soon became so haunted that to this day, residents have been known to flee the premises in the middle of the night, insisting that the ghosts just don't want them there.

There was, for instance, the night that four people decided to stay at the Stone House. One man slept in the apartment, a father and son shared the living room's sleeper sofa, and a young woman slept downstairs. In the middle of the night, the woman was awakened by the sound of footsteps upstairs. Thinking it was one of the other members of the group, she was about to go back to sleep when the footsteps became so thunderous that paint shavings began falling from the window ledge. Then the kitchen door suddenly slammed shut. The woman bolted from the house and slept in her car for the rest of the night. In the morning, when she told the others about her experience, they looked at her in bewilderment. None of them had been up and walking around at the time of the incident, and nobody had heard footsteps, or anything else out of the ordinary.

On another occasion, a couple named Al and Florence Jacobson heard inexplicable footsteps coming from the empty upstairs apartment, and saw a doorknob turn by itself. They also found objects moved during their absence.

One night, at around 1:00 a.m., a ranger who was staying at the Stone House awoke to the sight of someone sitting at the foot of his bed. He reached for his revolver. "I saw the shadowy figure of a soldier," he later reported. "His head and legs were missing. It was terrifying. He sat there for maybe a minute and then moved from the bed and disappeared into another room—through the wall!"

The ranger wasn't the only one who witnessed a phantom soldier. One evening an employee who was returning items to the storage area saw a shadowy figure in a dark corner. "He appeared to be a soldier," the employee recalled. "As I watched with disbelief, he walked right through the storage room's locked door."

The sound of knocking is a frequent paranormal occurrence at the Stone House. Two staff members were asleep in the room behind the locked door in the first-floor bedroom when one was awakened by loud bangs on the opposite side of the wall. He knew no one could have gotten in, because the doors were not only locked but had interior padlocks. When he called to his companion, the knocking stopped. When the two men had finally fallen back asleep, the knocking resumed. They never discovered the source of the eerie disturbance.

A strange knocking had a more sinister meaning for former ranger and Crow tribe member Mardell Plainfeather, who during her employment at the park reported encountering quite a few spirits, including two Sioux phantoms dressed for war on the battlefield. One night Plainfeather, who was living at the Stone House, heard three knocks at her bedroom door. She got up and opened the door, but no one was there. She checked on her children, but they were all asleep.

Plainfeather had a very uneasy feeling. According to Crow belief, three knocks heard in the night are a harbinger of death. The next day they learned that her husband's grandmother had died that night.

Perhaps the creepiest incident at the Stone House concerns Lieutenant Benjamin H. Hodgson, a member of the 7th Cavalry who died a horrible death near Reno Crossing. His leg shattered by a bullet that also killed his horse, Hodgson frantically attempted to crawl up a steep hill. But a Cheyenne arrow cut him down. He lay in agony for several hours until he finally died. His body rolled down to the riverbank, where a marker now stands.

One evening a woman named Christine Hope, who was staying at the Stone House, saw the apparition of a mustached man sitting at a table. He remained motionless for a minute or two, staring at her, before he vanished. Later, Hope came across a photo of Hodgson and identified him as the apparition she'd seen.

It's no question that the Battle of the Little Bighorn isn't over. Visitors and staff constantly witness ghostly remnants of the massacre—like the Vietnam veteran who in 1998 realized his long-cherished dream of finally visiting the site of

Custer's Last Stand. But almost immediately his excitement turned to dread. The feeling of "heaviness and sadness," he said, was everywhere. At the cemetery he sensed the presence of "others"—and not other tourists, either.

"I know this sounds crazy, but I started hearing voices," he recalled. "Now, I certainly wasn't one of those ghost hunters. I didn't know anything about the paranormal, and I'd never thought about it. But these voices were absolutely otherworldly. They were men's voices, quite a few of them. They were all whispering at the same time, and I couldn't make out what they were saying. But I knew they were very unhappy. Some were scared, others were in pain, others were really angry. They seemed to be talking to me, wanting me to do something for them. Then it gets even weirder. I began seeing shadowy shapes in my peripheral vision. Glimpses of men in dark uniforms, moving slowly towards me. But when I spun around to face them, there was no one there."

The Vietnam vet quickly left the cemetery and tried to put the unsettling experience out of his mind. But he was about to get an even bigger shock later in the day, when he and his wife visited Reno Crossing.

"The sounds started almost the moment we were close enough to the Little Bighorn to hear its waters flowing. Rifle fire, shouts, screams, and war whoops, all intermingling with the rushing of the river. Even though it was a bright and sunny day, as soon as we got to Reno Crossing, everything seemed to get darker and cooler. Then my heart stopped. There, on the other side of the river, was a soldier, an officer, I think. He had red hair and a short red beard. He just stood there, staring at me. He looked real sad, like he was saying goodbye for good, even though he didn't know who

I was. Then—it could have been a few seconds or a minute, although it seemed like time had stopped—he vanished."

It seems that the Crow Indians were only half right. Ghosts do indeed walk the earth at Little Bighorn, but not just in the hours between sunset and the first glimmers of dawn. The phantoms of Little Bighorn are apparently on duty at all hours of the day and night—including Custer himself, who, they say, resides at the park's museum and performs the real closing duties every night. But that leads us to our next story.

Chapter 21
General Custer and the Ghost Dance

During his short lifetime, he was dashing, arrogant, and rash—a daredevil who had eleven horses shot from under him and always went back for more. But in death, George Armstrong Custer is far less flamboyant. His ghost has appeared in various places, at various times, and always, witnesses say, he seems downcast, restless, and exceedingly disturbed—as if he is in perpetual mourning over the biggest mistake of his life.

Of all the ghosts at Little Bighorn Battlefield National Monument, the one people most expect to see is George Armstrong Custer's. And they haven't been disappointed. The general (he was actually a lieutenant colonel but has been accorded the title of general out of respect) has been seen wandering the battlefield in the buckskin clothing, bright red tie, and wide-brimmed campaign hat he was wearing on the day he died, and, on rare occasions, in the cemetery, where he appears for only a few seconds and then vanishes.

But the most frequent Custer sighting is at the park's museum. Employees making the rounds after closing time have reported seeing a transparent likeness of the general, strolling among the artifacts. This time he's dressed in his full military uniform and sports his long blond curls and handlebar mustache. He always looks sorrowful, and witnesses say his specter is accompanied by a sudden chill and a pervasive sense of dread.

Little Bighorn, however, isn't the only place Custer's ghost has been seen. There's a legend, as strange as it is poignant, that fourteen years after he died on that bloody Montana battlefield, the general made an appearance at the infamous Battle at Wounded Knee Creek, where he seemed to mourn along with the ghost of his old nemesis, Sitting Bull.

In an 1881 interview in the *New York Times*, Chief Sitting Bull explained how George Armstrong Custer had forced him into the famous battle that ended in the massacre of the U.S. 7th Cavalry.

"During the summer previous to the one in which Custer attacked us, he sent a letter to me telling me that if I did not go to an agency he would fight me, and I sent word back to him by his messenger that I did not want to fight, but only to be left alone. I told him at the same time that if he wanted to fight, he should go and fight those Indians who wanted to fight him.

"In the winter, Custer sent me word again. 'You would not take my former offer, now I am going to fight you this Winter.' I sent word back and said just what I had said before, that I did not want to fight and only wanted to be left alone, and that my camp was the only one that had not fought him. After some months, Custer again sent a message: 'I am fitting up my wagons and soldiers . . . I will fight you in eight days.'

"I then saw that it was no use, that I would have to fight, so I sent him word back. 'All right, get all your men mounted and I will get all my men mounted: we will have a fight. The Great Spirit will look on, and the side that is in the wrong will be defeated.'"

Thus was the Battle of Little Bighorn set in motion. Custer, notoriously full of himself, was determined to vanquish the Indians who refused to give up their sacred lands to the U.S. government. At thirty-six, he had visions of further greatness—some say the presidency—and knew that a victory over the formidable Sitting Bull and his fellow warrior chief, Crazy Horse, could propel him on that ambitious road. In her memoirs, *Boots and Saddles,* his wife, Elizabeth, described her dashing husband on the first day's march. "The lifting mist revealed a column almost two miles long. A bugle sounded 'Mount' and 'Forward,' and the procession moved out. My husband was buoyant at taking the field, his cavalry regiment platooned behind with guidons streaming. Infantry followed, then forty Indian scouts intoning their war dirge, pack mules, a battery of artillery, and a line of heavy white-hooded wagons."

Custer, as always, made a stirring figure, even without his trademark long yellow locks, which had earned him the name of "Yellow Hair" from the Native Americans. He had cut his hair and donned not a military uniform but a red tie, fringed buckskins, and a broad-brimmed campaign hat. He rode proudly atop his famous horse, Comanche, looking back to admire his command and never for a moment believing that he would not return to Elizabeth victorious. "He was sanguine," she wrote, "that but a few weeks would elapse before we would be reunited." But Mrs. Custer was not reassured. As the rising sun glimmered on the mist, she said, a mirage seemed to appear, of the 7th Cavalry riding on the clouds like ghostly horsemen in the sky. Her heart was heavy with foreboding; it seemed like nothing less than a premonition of disaster.

We all know the outcome of Custer's fatal pride. Elizabeth would never see her husband again. Within a matter of days, his body would lie dead on the bloodied prairie, alongside those of his maimed, scalped troops. God had not been on his side that day; in addition to the larger numbers and superior position of the Indians, a freak storm broke out just before Sitting Bull's men vanquished the cavalry. "The soldiers fired upon us as soon as we got within range," Sitting Bull recalled, "but did us little harm, even though we had got quite close to them. We were just going to charge them when a great storm broke right over us. The lightning was fearful, and struck a lot of the soldiers and horses, killing them instantly. I then called out to my men to charge the troops, and shouted out: 'The Great Spirit is on our side; look how he is striking the soldiers down!' So we charged them and we easily knocked them off their horses, and then killed them with our coup sticks."

Sitting Bull never personally saw Custer's body on the battlefield. But according to an odd and little known tale, the two men would meet once more, this time after death, at another famous battle between the U.S. Army and the Indians that would end in a terrible defeat for the Lakota Sioux. There is a legend—some swear it's a true story—that at the Battle at Wounded Knee Creek, the ghosts of both Sitting Bull and Yellow Hair appeared, not as adversaries but as brothers, reunited by the common bonds of shame and sorrow.

It all began with the Ghost Dance. A religious movement started by Paiute healer Wovoka—also known by his Anglo name, Jack Wilson—the Ghost Dance was a ritual that promised, at first, a nonviolent end to the white man's expansionism and a time of prosperity and peaceful coexistence among all peoples on the earth.

The Northern Piutes of Nevada, known as the Tovusidokado, were rapidly being reduced to starvation when Jack Wilson had an extraordinary vision on January 1, 1869. Foragers who survived on cypress bulbs, augmenting their diets with fish, pine nuts, and occasional wild game, the Piutes had a nomadic lifestyle that was gradually destroyed by a combination of Anglo encroachment on their lands and the introduction of various European diseases, particularly typhoid, that killed approximately one-tenth of the total population.

Wilson, who came from a line of Piute healers and "weather doctors," claimed that in his vision, he had stood before God in heaven. God showed him a beautiful land filled with wild game, where his ancestors were happily passing the time, and gave him the following instructions: "Return home and tell your people that they must love each other and live in peace with the whites. They must work hard; they must not steal or lie; and they must not engage in the old practices of war. If they abide by my rules, they will be united with all their loved ones in the next world." God then showed Wilson a powerful dance and commanded him to teach it to his people.

Wilson said he left the presence of God convinced that if every Indian in the West performed the new dance, all evil would cease and the earth would be cleansed to perfection. He immediately began preaching to the Piutes that if the five-day dance was performed properly, prosperity and happiness would prevail and the participants would soon be reunited in eternal bliss with their dead loved ones.

Wilson's message was your basic End of Days spiel, albeit with a happy ending for all, and it found a ready audience. The starving Piutes eagerly embraced anything that promised relief from the hell they were experiencing on earth. They quickly accepted the dance as virtually a new religion, calling it the "Dance in a Circle." The ritual soon spread to other tribes; the Sioux adopted it as the "Spirit Dance," and the white settlers gave it the name "Ghost Dance," because of the ghostly aura that presumably appeared around the dancers.

Jack Wilson was considered such a powerful prophet that he exerted a messianic influence over much of the western portion of the United States, winning over various Native American peoples as well as the Mormons in Utah, who, fond of prophets, found many of Wilson's teachings acceptable. But the Ghost Dance ran into trouble when it got into the hands of the Lakota Sioux, who twisted its original intention from a ritual of peace and nonviolence into, essentially, a war dance. When Wilson spoke of all evil being "washed away," the Sioux interpreted this to mean the removal of all Anglo-Americans from their lands, by force if necessary.

In February 1890, relations between the Sioux and the U.S. government deteriorated even further when the United States broke a Lakota treaty by reapportioning the Great Sioux Reservation of South Dakota into five smaller reservations to accommodate white homesteaders while "breaking up tribal relationships" and "converting the Indians to the white man's ways, peaceably if they will or forcibly if they must." This intolerable action was overseen by the Bureau of Indian Affairs. On cramped family plots, unable to cultivate crops in the arid region, and with the government cutting the Sioux rations in half to force the "lazy Indians" to work harder, the Sioux were on the verge of starvation. Performances of the

Ghost Dance started to increase, along with rage against the white oppressor, frightening the supervising BIA agents. Sitting Bull was accused of being the leader of the Ghost Dance movement, and thousands of extra U.S. Army troops were deployed to his reservation. The Sioux chief was ordered to stop his people from practicing the Ghost Dance; when he refused, he was arrested. During the arrest, an angry Sioux fired at one of the soldiers. The army troops retaliated and in the ensuing melee, Sitting Bull was killed.

Two weeks later, U.S. Army officers forced Miniconjou leader Big Foot, considered a troublemaker, to relocate his people to a small camp near the Pine Ridge Agency. On December 28, the small band of Sioux set up their tepees on the banks of Wounded Knee Creek. The following day, army officers were collecting weapons from them when one young warrior, who was deaf, could not understand what was going on. A struggle ensued, a weapon discharged into the air, and a U.S. officer gave the command to open fire. The Sioux grabbed their confiscated weapons but were decimated by the enemy's carbine firearms and rapid-fire light artillery. The unplanned Battle at Wounded Knee Creek left 25 U.S. soldiers dead, many of whom were killed by friendly fire, and massacred 153 Sioux, mostly women and children.

On that horrible day, amidst the weeping, screaming, and wailing, it's said that the ghost of Sitting Bull appeared, to grieve with his people. It's also said that the ghost of George Armstrong Custer was seen as well. Some assumed that he had somehow been behind the slaughter, to settle the score of Little Bighorn. But others reported that he seemed anything but triumphant. In fact, he had a mournful expression, as if he were commiserating with his old adversary.

Had the Ghost Dance somehow been successful in conjuring up the two rival spirits and uniting them in peace? Whether there's any credence to this tale, we'll never know. But we do know that Custer's ghost does seem to get around. In addition to his regular appearances at the Little Bighorn Monument, he's also been sighted in Kansas, at his old home in Fort Riley, where he resided with Elizabeth and the 7th Cavalry in 1866 and 1867, as well as at several of his former residences. He has also, they say, been known to throw a temper tantrum or two; one tourist at Little Bighorn reported the following eerie incident.

"It was a chilly but calm day. As we started walking up the hill to the actual site of Custer's Last Stand, my son asked me why General Custer didn't wait for reinforcements when he heard about the size of the Indian village. I told him, 'Because Custer was vain and arrogant.'

"Suddenly, an icy wind came from nowhere and started gusting wildly across the prairie. My hat blew right off my head and flew into an embankment. I had to chase it for fifty yards. The wind never let up for the rest of our visit. I swear, it was the ghost of George Armstrong Custer!"

But perhaps the most unusual report of a Custer sighting came from San Francisco freelance writer Jeremy Russell, who was in the Custer Battlefield Trading Post, a gift shop near the entrance to the park, when he found a postcard inscribed with the words "The spirit of General George A. Custer returns in a puff of smoke!"

"Taken at what appears to be dawn," wrote Russell, "the picture on the card is of a plume of smoke that has a startling resemblance to Custer.

"'Isn't that amazing?' the cashier said. 'The woman who took that photograph took it from right over here. There was a grass fire in the battlefield back in 1996, and she thought she was just taking a picture of the smoke plume. When it was developed and she showed it to a friend, he asked her, 'Where'd you get that picture of General Custer?' Then she started showing it to a lot of people, and this one guy bought it and made the postcard.'

"She paused for a moment to look at the picture. 'It's kind of spooky.' She shook her head. 'Isn't it?'"

Part Seven

SOME STORIES FROM WHERE AMERICANS FOUGHT ABROAD

Chapter 22

The Restless Spirits
of Normandy Beach

On June 6, 1944, Allied forces invaded the beaches of Normandy, in the first phase of D-day. A huge number of the initial wave of infantrymen perished in a confused rush to escape waiting German fire. Today, sixty-four years later, many say their ghosts still haunt the Omaha and Utah beaches, as well as the surrounding countryside, and locals have learned to live with the disquieting feeling of "always being watched."

The invasion of Normandy, the Allied effort that launched D-day, was the largest seaborne invasion in history, involving over three million troops crossing the English Channel from England to Normandy in occupied France. Twelve allied nations provided fighting units that participated in the invasion. D-day began on June 6, 1944, with an assault phase known as Operation Neptune, aimed at establishing a secure foothold on the Normandy beaches.

The task was daunting, of a magnitude never before attempted in military history. General Dwight Eisenhower would have to move his forces one hundred miles across the English Channel and storm a heavily fortified coastline, defended by the crack German army, commanded by the brilliant General Erwin Rommel. The superiority of the Germans' weapons, particularly their tanks, was well known. In addition, Rommel's seasoned troops would be an intimidating match for the green young Americans, many of whom had never even seen combat.

It had been 256 years since an invading army had crossed the perilous English Channel. The Allies were at even more of a disadvantage because their 5,000-vessel armada was anything but inconspicuous. Add to that 4,000 smaller landing craft and over 11,000 aircraft and a covert operation was doubly precarious. Nonetheless, on June 6, the Allies made it to the Utah and Omaha beachheads and, by sheer force of numbers, secured French coastal villages. Reinforcements came pouring in, and by June 11, more than 326,000 troops, 55,000 vehicles, and 100,000 tons of supplies had arrived. By July, the Allies were firmly entrenched in Normandy and the liberation of France had begun.

But June 6, 1944, would forever remain a day of horror for the American, British, and Canadian troops who, when they neared the Normandy coast, were suddenly attacked by the waiting Germans strategically positioned atop the jagged cliffs overlooking the Channel. It was chaos. As the enemy barrage began, soldiers scrambled willy-nilly to reach the shore and were shot either in the water or as soon as they reached land. They were essentially sitting ducks, in full view of the "Heinies," who picked them off with deadly precision. Their plans in disarray, the Allies' only chance was to try to outrun the fuselage and find cover anywhere they could. By nightfall, the carnage had temporarily ended in 9,000 dead and wounded, and by the time D-day operations were complete, the Allies had sustained some 210,000 casualties. Even though the operation was finally successful, the terrible cost of victory could never be forgotten.

Years later, one veteran of the first doomed wave of Operation Neptune, Thomas Valence of Company A, 116th Infantry Regiment, U.S. 29th Division, recalled his experience.

"I came down the ramp, in water pretty much knee high, and started to do what we were trained to do—go forward, crouch down, and fire. The only problem was, we didn't know exactly what to fire at. I saw some tracers coming from a concrete emplacement that looked mammoth; I didn't ever anticipate any gun emplacements being that big. So I fired at that. I had no concept of what was going on behind me; there was not much to see in front of me, and the water kept coming in so rapidly and the fellows I was with were being hit so rapidly that it became a struggle to stay on one's feet. What I did was to abandon my equipment, which was very heavy and tended to weigh us down. It was evident rather quickly that we weren't going to accomplish very much that day.

"I remember floundering in the water with my hand up in the air, trying to get my bearings, when I was first shot, through the hand, in the finger and palm. Next to me in the water, a fellow named Hank Witt was rolling over toward me and I remember very clearly him saying, 'Sergeant, they're leaving us here to die like rats. Just like rats.'

"Now, I didn't necessarily share his opinion; I didn't know whether we'd been abandoned or not, or really what was going on. But it turns out that he had extraordinary insight. Subsequent waves did not come in behind us, as was planned originally. I made my way forward and was hit several other times, once in the thigh, breaking the bone. I worked my way onto the beach and staggered up against a wall and pretty much collapsed there in that position for the remainder of the day. Meanwhile, the bodies of the other guys began washing ashore, many of which had been severely blown to pieces. It was not a very pleasant way to spend a day. I don't recall any other troops coming in that day. Essentially my part of the invasion had ended, with most of my company having been wiped out.

"I've wondered over the years why we in Company A of the First Battalion, 116th Infantry, 29th Division were chosen to be the American equivalent of storm troopers. Was it because we were so highly trained? Because we had such potential? Actually, we'd had no combat duty, and no other troops were with us. Or was it because we were simply considered expendable?"

The terrible, many believe needless, slaughter of so many young Allied troops left its grim aftermath, in both the memories of the survivors and the persistent psychic phenomena that have been reported on the beaches and in the villages of Normandy. There is, for instance, the story of the "Ghost of the 116th," Thomas Valence's regiment, told by a young girl who was visiting Normandy in the summer of 1999 with her grandmother.

"I went to France with my grandma in 1999. We went to Normandy to see all the villages there and the place where D-day occurred. At Omaha Beach, we went to the cemetery and I was shocked. I couldn't believe so many people died on one single beach. Later that night, my grandma was awakened by a deep male voice that kept on repeating, 'Help me . . . help me . . . my leg . . .' Then it would stop. I didn't understand why the spirit was in our hotel room. The second night, my grandma was awakened again and this time she said she saw the person clearly. She said he was a captain, he was in the 116th division and was part of the first wave to hit the beach. He lost his leg when he was going up the beach. He was hit by a mortar and then was shot in the head. I asked how she could know all that stuff and she said, 'He told me.' From that day on, I was scared stiff."

Ask any resident of the Normandy countryside and he or she will tell you that *bien sur, les fantomes sont encore ici*. The ghosts of Normandy have become accepted as part of the landscape, just one more tragic reminder of the war that so shattered their lives.

On June 4, 1994—fifty years after the onset of D-day— two American tourists—we'll call them Larry and Anne— visited Omaha Beach. It was around 7 p.m., they recalled, and they had decided to take a leisurely walk when they heard what distinctly sounded like German voices barking out orders. This was followed by the sound of machine-gun fire. Larry and Anne fell in the sand. As Larry was getting up, he stuck his hand into the sand and grabbed a handful of spent rounds.

It turned out they weren't the only ones who had heard the machine guns. Some other visitors had also hit the deck in terror. One called the authorities, who came out to investigate. By this time a small crowd had gathered. "We could still hear the machine guns and German soldiers shouting out orders," said Anne, "but this time it seemed fainter, as if coming from a greater distance. After a while, a few of the veterans of the Omaha Beach assault came down near the beach and pointed out the German machine-gun positions. They, too, could hear the phantom gunfire, and they said it was coming from just where the Germans had been stationed that day so long ago."

Eventually the authorities returned from their investigation. They'd found nothing, they said. But they did tell the terrified tourists that the spirits of the dead are walking the earth. "They are playing their tricks on you," said one of the police officers. And he wasn't joking.

Later the next day, locals living in and around Normandy told Larry and Anne that they saw and heard strange things all the time, like gunfire, shouts, moans, and cries, and that it was not unusual to see ghosts of Allied and German soldiers walking the beaches. One old woman who lived through the invasion recalled the day an engine fire on one of the Tiger 1 tanks set off the ammunition stores, killing the crew and destroying her house. "The Germans rebuilt my house," she said. "But the ghost of the Tiger and its crew, they are still in my backyard. Many times I hear the rumble of the tank, turning over its engine."

Most of the residents, she said, stay away from the beaches. "We feel like we are being watched," she explained. And in the town of Normandy, the spirits are apparently even bolder. Many witnesses claim that they have seen Allied soldiers dressed for the invasion, walking down the streets in broad daylight.

If so many witnesses, both resident and tourist, are to be believed, many of the soldiers who perished in Normandy still remain there. A member of the military had an eerie experience with the undead during a re-creation of a paratrooper maneuver, on the occasion of the fortieth anniversary of D-day.

"In 1984, I was serving with the 82nd Airborne Division out of Fort Bragg and had the opportunity to participate in the fortieth D-day anniversary, which involved a task force from our division jumping first into the U.K. and linking with the British Parachute Regiment and then with some of them joining us, turning around and jumping onto our old combat drop zones around St. Mère Église, which was the first town liberated by the Allies on the European mainland during World War II. This was the first time a unit from the 82nd had returned to Normandy and on 5 June, 1984, we jumped into a drop zone by parachute that was just a few miles east of St. Mère Église, between the town and the Utah landing beaches. We were then bused over to a location known as Timme's Orchards, where a regimental commander of the 507th Parachute Regiment had started his fight after landing there.

"After arriving that evening, we made arrangements to sleep outside in the farm orchard. After dark, we held a memorial service at midnight, complete with the playing of taps. One of our chaplains told us that forty years ago, at that moment, American paratroopers were quietly descending upon the very spot where we were standing. I had the absolutely disquieting feeling that they were still there, that we definitely weren't alone.

"Then, out of the corner of my eye, I saw a misty shape, in the trees to the right of me. I turned and saw the figure of a soldier in a paratrooper's uniform. He flickered there for a minute or so. Although the moon was out, and it could have been just moonlight, he seemed to be bathed in a soft light. I blinked, and when I opened my eyes he was still there. I turned to the guy next to me, to ask him if he could see him, but when my buddy looked over into the trees, there was nothing there. Was it my imagination, sparked by the chaplain's story? Or had I really seen a ghost? To this day I'm not sure, but if you pinned me to the wall, I'd have to say it was the latter. I feel, deep down, that one of the men who died in that area had made a brief appearance—one which I'll never forget."

Perhaps the most moving account of spirit sightings comes from a recent widower who was visiting Normandy in an effort to get away from home and its attendant grief.

"I went to Omaha Beach with a group of remarkable men, men who had been there before as part of the Allied invasion force into Normandy and now, for various reasons, had returned to recall that experience. One of these, Merwin Hams, was a navy lieutenant in charge of six landing craft that put hundreds of soldiers on Omaha Beach on the morning of June 6, 1944. He was traveling alone, as I was, and we had become travel companions. In the fifty-four years since that June day, Merwin had put that experience out of his mind. But now, he felt, it was important to bring it all back.

"When we arrived, Merwin slipped away from our group and walked by himself far out on the beach to the water's edge. I saw him there, standing alone, and walked across that long stretch of beach to join him.

"When I approached, I saw that he was crying and staring at the sand around him. He saw me and beckoned me to join him.

"'I see bodies,' he whispered.

"'Where?' I asked.

"'Everywhere.' He made a sweeping motion with his arm. 'They are stretched from here all the way to the bluff.'

"Merwin told me that on that foggy morning in 1944, he had been directed to land his boats at a point directly in line with a small church located near what was called the 'gap,' the thin break in the bluffs that would be the only way off Omaha Beach that day. But he never saw the church, he said, so he put his boats and their cargo here, where we stood. The next thing they knew, the Germans were firing on them. He lost most of his men.

"It was all coming back, and I think that was why he had come here, alone, to stand with the ghosts. But then he said an incredible thing. 'I see bodies,' he said. 'But over there, near the bluffs today, I see children playing in the sand.'

"His eyes cleared and then he smiled. 'That's what I'll take home with me. I'll remember that children are playing today in the sand on Omaha Beach.'"

And so, life goes on, for both the living and the dead.

Chapter 23
The Ghosts
of Corregidor

The Philippine stronghold of Corregidor was the site of terrible losses, both American and Japanese, during World War II. To this day, the island is reputedly haunted by phantoms from both armies, some benign, some vicious, as well as other victims of war. Among the most legendary of Corregidor's ghosts are the "Mad Nurse of Corregidor" and the terrifying "Faceless Phantom," who is said to haunt the Corregidor Hotel.

All that is known of her is that she was a Filipino nurse who fell in love with an American serviceman in 1942. As often as they could, the couple would meet under a giant narra tree in front of a bomb shelter, where they would snatch whatever desperate embraces time allowed.

One night, the story goes, the serviceman failed to show up. His bewildered and heartbroken girlfriend could not believe she'd been stood up. In truth, her lover had died in action that day. But she never found out because, overwhelmed with rage and depression, she killed herself a few days later.

But that doesn't mean this nurse left terra firma. To this day, people say, an insane woman, clad in a nursing uniform of the 1940s, can be seen roaming about the old bomb shelter grounds with a syringe and an insane look in her eyes. On the anniversary of her lover's death, her ghost is believed to appear under the narra tree, which still stands to this day.

Fact or fiction? Given the many reports of prodigious paranormal activity on Corregidor, it behooves one to think twice before dismissing the "Mad Nurse" as merely the product of imagination in overdrive. To those familiar with the island, she's just one of many spectral entities who seem to have unfinished business, a score to settle, perhaps, or a last, pressing duty to attend to before she can finally rest in peace.

Of all the battlefields of World War II, perhaps none had so many brutal twists and turns as Corregidor, the island bastion that was vital in the conquest of the Philippines. Corregidor was the site of two particularly bloody battles—the Japanese won the first, in 1942, but the second, in 1945, ended in an Allied victory and recapture of the island. Officially named Fort Mills, Corregidor was the largest of four islands protecting the mouth of Manila Bay from attack. To the Americans, it was known as "The Rock" and the "Gibraltar of the East."

Corregidor had an extensive network of tunnels, the most famous being Manila Tunnel, the headquarters of General Douglas MacArthur. This tunnel was a virtual bomb-proofed underground city, with reinforced concrete walls and floors, an overhead electric tramway line along the east-west passage, a hospital, a storehouse, and even shops. Today Manila Tunnel is reputed to be the most haunted site on Corregidor.

Before the Americans could even catch their breath from the Pearl Harbor attack that launched the United States' entrance into the war, the Japanese began an aerial bombardment of Corregidor on December 29, 1941, that demolished many key strongholds.

On March 12, 1942, General MacArthur was evacuated from Corregidor in the dead of night and taken by PT boat to Mindanao. From there he relocated to Australia, where he continued to command the Philippine defenses. But his orders during the fierce siege of April–May 1942—a result of ignorance and arrogance—ended up imperiling the lives of his own men.

From January to April 1942, the troops on the Bataan Peninsula suffered constantly from hunger and disease. At one point they even cooked and ate their own mules. When the Japanese renewed their offensive on April 3, 1942, the American survivors were so weakened that they could not offer any effective resistance. Nonetheless, from faraway Australia, where he was comfortably ensconced in his new headquarters, MacArthur ordered a general counterattack against the Japanese, ignoring the dismal condition of his abandoned troops and a severe shortage of military supplies that essentially made their position untenable.

The commanding officer on Luzon, Major General Edward King, chose to ignore MacArthur's directive and surrendered his troops on April 9, 1942, hoping that they would be treated with European-style decency as POWs. Instead the Japanese subjected the sick and exhausted American troops to humiliation, the horrific Bataan Death March, and the intolerable conditions of the Japanese "hell camps."

Meanwhile, on Corregidor, General Jonathan Wainwright obeyed MacArthur and continued the futile fight. The eleven thousand courageous defenders of the island resisted intense Japanese bombardment that left them sleepless for days. In a twenty-four-hour-period, over twelve thousand shells exploded; "even huddled deep underground in the Manila Tunnel," said one report, "women and children bled from the ears from the concussive effect produced by the earth-shaking explosions overhead." Finally, on May 6, out of food, ammunition, and water, Wainwright surrendered to the Japanese, in the hopes of avoiding reprisals against his troops and the women and children under his care. But instead, as on Bataan, the Japanese subjected their captives to cruel imprisonment or execution.

The Americans had their revenge in 1945, when they retook Corregidor. This time it was the Japanese who suffered terrible losses. Many loyal soldiers of the emperor elected to commit suicide rather than face the shame of capture. But instead of ending their own lives, did they simply prolong them into eternity?

The entire island of Corregidor is considered a World War II battleground, and ghosts have been reported all over the area. Since the end of World War II, visitors to Corregidor's tunnels have been reporting strange occurrences. In the ruins of the old hospital, footsteps are frequently heard, along with bustling hospital activity and eerie moans and cries. Inside the tunnels where Japanese soldiers blew themselves up, mysterious orbs—inexplicable balls of light associated with ghosts and spirits—have appeared to many eyewitnesses and have even been captured on film. One psychic who was called in to examine photographs of the orbs taken inside the Manila Tunnel proclaimed the site "a house of spirits that never go away."

According to paranormal research, orbs are energies of spirits or ghosts who have existed physically. "The spirits manifest themselves either in human form or as a small orb," the psychic said. Areas with a heightened degree of static energy—such as tunnels, for instance—are prime places for orbs to manifest. And in areas of not only high static but also high emotional energy, ghosts definitely leave their imprints.

In other photographs, mysterious figures sometimes appear. The Filipino magazine *People Today* printed one such photo taken in the "hospital tunnel," in which two blurred male figures are visible. One appears to be a soldier in uniform, in a half-kneeling position, wearing a hat with a cloth attached to it. The other figure looks like a patient sitting on the lower portion of a bunk bed. Could he be one of the patients from sixty years before, who just happened to never check out?

Although technology experts usually debunk images of orbs caught on camera as merely deflection of lights, ghostly figures like the soldier and patient are not nearly so easy to dismiss. Neither is the story of the "Faceless Phantom," a malevolent entity who reputedly haunts the lovely Corregidor Hotel. No one knows for sure who or what this being is, and no one wants to get close enough to find out. One hotel guest did get too close for comfort to the Phantom, and her story is truly a tale of terror.

Lida (not her real name) was a twenty-two-year-old nursing student living in Manila who decided to take an overnight trip to Corregidor with some of her schoolmates. It was supposed to be a fun camping trip, but it turned into a living nightmare when Lida and two other classmates decided to stay at the Corregidor Hotel instead.

After an exhilarating day exploring the beautiful island, the girls returned to their room. While Lida's friends relaxed on one bed, sharing girl talk, Lida stretched out on the other bed. That's when things took a wrong turn.

"I wasn't tired yet," Lida recalled, "and I hadn't planned to fall asleep. But as I closed my eyes, I had this strange feeling like something had changed. Something was wrong. The rest will sound very strange, but I don't know how else to explain or describe it.

"The very moment I closed my eyes, the room shifted. It was as though I still had my eyes open. The real difference was the color of light. It was a purplish shade or haze that now filled the room.

"I could see the two girls sitting on the other bed talking. I was lucid. Everything was very vivid. This wasn't a dream. Confused, I slowly turned my head to look around. That's when I noticed a shape. I thought it to be the outline of a man standing near my bed, although it was more like a dark mass. A man without features. The rest happened very fast. When I realized the form was there, it reacted to me. First it seemed surprised that I had seen it. Then it lunged at me. I sat straight up and put my arms in front of me to fight off my attacker. At the moment we touched, I woke to my own screams and my roommates rushing to my side.

"The color of the light in the room returned to normal. The 'thing' was gone—but there was a soreness on both my arms from where it had grabbed me. I was deeply frightened but didn't tell the girls what I had seen. I was afraid they'd tell me I'd been asleep and that it was all a nightmare, and I knew in my heart it had not been a dream. I was so disturbed that I spent the night with some friends in the next room.

"The next day, as I waited to board the ferry back to Manila with the rest of the group, one of the girls from my shared room came up to me. I could tell something was bothering her, but she was reluctant to tell me what it was.

On the long boat ride back to Manila, she broke down and told me about the nightmare she had had. She dreamed she wrestled with an angry and violent intruder who tried to throw her from the bed. The most horrible thing about this creature was that it had no face. During the fight, the room was bathed in a strange light. She said it was like seeing in the darkness with only the light from a very bright, full moon, but in a purple color.

"That's when I told her why I had sat up in bed screaming with my arms in front of me. She began to cry and kept nodding her head 'Yes!' when I told her about the dark shape with no face."

Who or what is this malevolent entity? An angry Japanese or American soldier who died in combat and will take revenge on anybody who crosses its path? A civilian war casualty who's determined to make somebody pay for his agony? Perhaps it's Lieutenant General Masaharu Homma, commander of the 14th Japanese Imperial Army, who was unceremoniously relieved of his command during the first Battle for Corregidor and has come back to vent his rage. Or could it be Douglas MacArthur himself, still cranky about his embarrassment over the fall of the island and determined not to fade away just yet?

Chapter 24
The Ghosts
of Pearl Harbor

The sounds of bombing, ghosts dressed in WWII army fatigues, a spirit who still has a message for the folks back home—these are just a few of the reported instances of heavy paranormal activity at Pearl Harbor, where nearly 2,500 U.S. servicemen lost their lives in the infamous attack that led to our entrance into World War II. Among the most haunted locations on the island are Hickam Air Force Base and the USS Arizona. *And perhaps the most fascinating of all the apparitions who have been sighted are the "Two Charleys."*

The Hawaiians call it *mana*—the life force that remains in a person's bones after death. All over the islands there are *helaus,* shelters built to house the bones of the deceased and save the mana. Yet even though there are no helaus per se on Oahu's Ford Island, the small island in the center of Pearl Harbor and the Naval Complex, the mana seems to be everywhere. Residents have reported strange occurrences, such as ghostly voices and footsteps, objects mysteriously moved or stacked, lights and appliances suddenly turning on at night, and a pale, glowing foglike apparition that floats through their houses. Some have also seen misty figures of men in uniform, walking amid the buildings and trees on the north side of the island. These apparitions always vanish within seconds, only to return in time for the next observer.

Welcome to haunted Pearl Harbor.

It was an "unbelievably gorgeous" December morning in Hawaii, Hugh Roper remembered. "I'll never forget the smell of flowers in the air. I'd gotten up early that day for church. I was coming out of the mess hall in the barracks when I noticed a crowd had gathered. I looked up into the sky and saw Japanese bombers. Then I heard the first explosion. Pearl Harbor was under attack."

The Japanese surprise attack on the U.S. Pacific Fleet was a resounding success. The planes came in two waves; the first hit its target at 7:53 a.m., the second at 8:55. Looking back on the event that shocked the world, it bears a chilling resemblance to another "day that shall live in infamy," 9/11.

By 9:55 a.m. on December 7, 1941, the nefarious mission had been accomplished and the carriers that launched the bombers from 274 miles off the coast of Oahu were headed home to Japan. In their wake, they left the shattered remains of the U.S. defenses in Hawaii—2,403 men lay dead, 188 planes were destroyed, and the American Pacific Fleet had been crippled. The back of the USS *Arizona* was broken in a devastating explosion. The *Oklahoma* rolled over and was never returned to service. The battleships *Nevada, West Virginia,* and *California* all sank but were repaired and active again by 1943. Only the *Maryland* and *Tennessee* survived with moderate to serious damage.

"Battleship Row" was the main target of the attack's first wave. The *Arizona* was the first hit. The explosion has been described as ripping the ship's sides open "like a tin can." As Marine Corporal E. C. Nightingale recalled years later, "At approximately eight o'clock on the morning of December 7, 1941, I was leaving the breakfast table when the ship's siren for air defense sounded. Suddenly I heard an explosion. I ran to the port door leading to the quarterdeck and saw a bomb strike a barge of some sort alongside the Nevada. . . . I was about three-quarters of the way to the first platform on the mast when it seemed as though a bomb struck our quarterdeck. I could hear shrapnel or fragments whistling past me. Then I saw Second Lieutenant Simonson lying on his back with blood on his shirtfront. I bent over him and, taking him by the shoulders, asked if there was anything I could do, but he was dead.

"I had just arrived in secondary aft when a terrible explosion caused the ship to shake violently. I looked at the boat deck and everything seemed aflame. The major ordered us to leave, and I made my way to the quay. The bodies of the dead were thick; charred bodies were everywhere."

Corporal Nightingale was one of the few survivors of the attack on the *Arizona*. But more than a few spirit survivors apparently remain on duty aboard their old battleship. Visitors to the USS *Arizona* Memorial have encountered voices and footsteps in empty rooms, eerie lights and orbs, and the disquieting apparition of a horribly burned sailor who still walks the decks in silent agony. The sounds of the actual bombing are also said to be audible, playing over and over again in an eternal continuous loop. And one of the strangest instances of the unexplained is that sixty-seven years after the *Arizona* was destroyed, oil droplets still bubble from her remains, as if her battered corpse still breathes.

A psychic who calls herself Bella had a particularly intense experience at the *Arizona* Memorial.

"It was one of the most beautiful days of my life. The skies were such a pretty shade of blue, with big fluffy white clouds floating above, just scattered enough to accent the sunlight. As I visited the memorial at Pearl Harbor on the island of Oahu, I seemed to be the only one aware of the many hundreds of spirits calling out to anyone who could see them. The heavy sadness there broke my heart and seemed so at opposites with the peaceful day.

"There is a beautifully landscaped wall that borders the water of the harbor from the welcome station. My first sense that the spirits were strong there was when I turned to watch my granddaughters at play and I saw the pixilated lights dancing near a palm tree. I knew that a spirit was coming forward. As I waited for that brief minute for the contact that I have learned means some spirit has sensed my ability and is trying to talk to me, more distortions began to appear all around me and I began hearing desperate whisperings. I tried to slow them down, but these spirits were so eager to get news to their loved ones, and to tell me about them, that I couldn't take it all in. The pressure on me mounted, and the longer I stayed, the worse it got. While thankfully most of those souls that died at Pearl Harbor have moved on, some are still trapped, either by their fears of an after-life or the need to finish some important business. Or they may simply have left behind a residual energy imprinted on the area at the time of their passing."

Bella says she was able to get a few "personal contacts"— actual names and information—and cites in particular a young man named Red, who was particularly pushy.

"He was very sweet, but he rushed me because he was so anxious to get a message to his sweetheart back home in the Midwest. I told him she was no longer here and had recently passed away, and I truly felt she was waiting for him to come through. My daughter-in-law, who was with me, explained that if he was enlisted military, I should tell him to 'in-process.' When I followed her instruction, Red clearly understood its meaning and became much more at peace. I was so happy to be able to help at least one spirit there."

Ever since the Japanese attack, a ghost fondly referred to as "Charley" has haunted the halls of Pearl Harbor's Hickam Air Force Base. In 1941, Hickam was the largest building in the U.S. military, acting as a dorm for 3,200 men on December 7, 1941. More than 60 soldiers, most of them eating breakfast, died at the Pacific Air Forces headquarters building that day.

One of those casualties might have been Charley. Staff and visitors to Hickam have heard the sound of loud footsteps and keys jangling in the empty hallways. A janitor watched in disbelief as a faucet in one of the bathrooms suddenly turned on by itself. Even a sergeant turned tail and ran out of the building when some heavy glass doors opened by some unseen hand and began furiously swinging back and forth.

Whenever people report the eerie happenings, they're given the usual response: "Oh, that's just Charley."

Hickam deputy command historian Bill Harris admitted that Hickam is a spooky place, in large part because of Charley. Even though Harris is anything but a certified believer in ghosts, "I'm not going to say he's not out there," he said.

But guess what? The U.S. Navy apparently has two Charleys.

The decommissioned USS *Lexington* aircraft carrier, now a permanently harbored floating museum in Corpus Christi,

Texas, was once a proud battleship that served with distinction during World War II. It was nicknamed the "Blue Ghost" because it somehow survived four attacks by the Japanese Navy and was thought to be the ship that continued to return from the grave. At several points during the war, the *Lexington* was stationed at Pearl Harbor.

The *Lexington's* Charley—spelled in this case "Charly"—is a bona fide ghost who has made himself not only visible but also helpful to visitors. He's described as a blue-eyed, blond-haired young seaman in a spanking-white uniform who tells stories about the ship to those who are touring it. The phantom docent is extremely knowledgeable; one of the actual tour guides, a former airman on the *Lexington,* says Charly has revealed information about the ship that even he didn't know.

Charly has been identified as a former crew member who died during a Japanese kamikaze attack in 1944, off the coast of the Philippines. On the Corpus Christi *Caller-Times* Web site, over two hundred visitors to the museum have reported encountering him. Time and time again, they describe him as a "polite young man" who seems to be extraordinarily familiar with the ship's engine room. In fact, there have been so many Charly sightings in the engine room that a "ghost cam" has been installed there, to chart his movements twenty-four hours a day.

Sometimes Charly prefers to remain invisible. Museum Director of Operations M. Charles Reustle says that on several occasions, he's heard clothes rustling and footsteps following him. But when he turned around, no one was there. And on one amazing afternoon, a painting and restoration crew had taken a break, only to return and find that the project they'd been working on had been mysteriously finished for them.

Like Casper the Friendly Ghost, Charly seems ready and willing to be of service to all. In life, he must have been one heck of a seaman. As for his counterpart at Hickam Air Force Base, well, he's more mischievous than helpful, although still anything but sinister. Sometimes, it seems, a ghost can be a good thing—or at least not a bad one.

Chapter 25
The Organ-Playing Ghost Who Saved Two Yanks

We've all heard stories of ghostly organists, whose sinister playing usually signals doom for anyone who hears it. But we'll end our book on literally a happy note, with the story of two young American soldiers who, during World War II, got separated from their unit and took refuge in a mysterious old castle with a very unusual organ.

One of the most popular elements in ghost stories is the "haunted organ." Why this instrument is so popular among the spectral set is a mystery, although, with its massive power and strong connection to churches, cathedrals, and other spiritual sites, an organ definitely provides an effective medium for ghosts to be heard and to get their message across to everybody, in this world and the next.

Haunted organs have been reported all over the world. At Carbisdale Castle in Scotland, there's apparently a multi-talented spirit who plays both the organ and bagpipes. The pipes can be heard coming from underneath the castle, and ghostly organ music has been heard in the castle ballroom.

In New Haven, Connecticut, Yale University is proud of its haunted organ. Students and staff alike have reported hearing phantom music coming from the old organ in Woolsey Hall.

And then there's the popular legend about a church in Knoxville, Tennessee, that supposedly housed the haunted organ of organs. The story goes that in the early 1900s, a certain aging organ builder was contracted to build a magnificent instrument that would be his last. When it was finally completed, he asked the famous organist who was to inaugurate it to perform the Bach choral prelude "Christ Lay in the Bonds of Death." The conceited organist refused, and that night the old builder died suddenly. The following day, just as the great organist was about to begin his recital, the organ suddenly began playing the prelude all by itself. Everyone bolted from the church, to the sound of "Christ Lay in the Bonds of Death" and the maniacal laughter of the ghostly organist.

Now, these stories are probably apocryphal, the stuff of hearsay and urban legend. But there is one haunted organ story that seems to have some substance. It's told by a man whose father told it to him, and it's more than a little convincing.

"This is a ghost story that my father told me when he was a soldier in World War II. Dad was a corporal in General Patton's army. One day, as they were marching their way across Europe, Dad and one of his best friends, Sweeney, got separated from their unit during some heavy exchanges with the Germans. The unit was scattered as they sought cover from incoming shelling. When it was over, they could not find their way back to their unit.

"As darkness settled in, a steady rain began to fall. Dad and Sweeney decided to hole up in one of the many abandoned bombed-out buildings scattered along the road. They came to this one building, which Dad said looked like a mini-castle, and ducked in out of the rain to rest. They figured they would continue their search for their unit when the light of dawn came.

"Both men did a quick inspection of the place to verify that they were alone. There was scattered furniture, broken crates, boxes, and other clutter on the floor, and huge holes in the walls and ceiling where bombs had hit their target. The only thing that wasn't completely destroyed was an old pipe organ standing in the far corner of the room.

"As they opened their food rations, they heard a sound coming from where the organ was. Dad went over to investigate. Nothing was out of the ordinary. They chalked it up to fatigue and imagination. As they sat back down, they heard the sound again. This time it was music. 'It's the damn organ playing!' said Sweeney. They went over to the organ and saw the keys moving up and down and heard the music playing. Sweeney thought at first that it was a player piano–type organ, but upon further inspection, they discovered that there were no guts to the organ. The insides of the wood cabinet had been shredded to bits. There was no way that organ could be playing. Yet, there they were, listening and watching the ghostly performance.

"'I'm getting the hell out of here!' Sweeney said. 'There's a ghost in here, and he doesn't want us around!' Both men raced out of the castle and down the road. Miraculously, a few minutes later, they ran right into their unit.

"'You guys were really lucky to have found us,' the captain said. 'We'd switched course and were heading north.' Dad and Sweeney looked at each other, realizing that if they hadn't left the castle when they did and had waited until morning, the unit would have been long gone and they would have been left behind enemy lines, and more than likely captured. The ghostly organist had saved their lives."

Selected Bibliography

In addition to the dozens of stories I found online, there are some key publications and Web sites I'd like to acknowledge here.

Books

Asfar, Dan, *Haunted Battlefields* (2004, Ghost House Books).

Belanger, Jeff, *Ghosts of War: Restless Spirits of Soldiers, Spies and Saboteurs* (2006, Career Press).

Coleman, Christopher A., *Ghosts and Haunts of the Civil War* (1999, Rutledge Hill Press).

Cottrell, Steve, *Haunted Ozarks Battlefields: Civil War Ghost Stories and Brief Battle Histories* (2007, Two Trails Publishing).

Hamlin, Marie Caroline, *Legends of Le Detroit* (1883, T. Nourse).

McPherson, James M., *Battle Cry of Freedom: The Civil War Era* (1988, Oxford University Press).

Nesbitt, Mark and Patty A. Wilson, *Haunted Pennsylvania: Ghosts and Strange Phenomena of the Keystone State* (2006, Stackpole Books).

Wlodarski, Robert and Anne Powell Wlodarski, *Spirits of the Alamo* (1999, Republic of Texas Press).

Newspaper

"An Interview with Sitting Bull," *The New York Times,* April 3, 1881.

Web sites

Audio account of Normandy Invasion, Thomas Valence, Company A, 116th Infantry Regiment, found on *D-Day Web: The Real Normandy,* linked to *the Encyclopædia Britannica.*

"Beardslee Castle Ghosts," from Georgia Ghost Hunters blog, www.georgia-ghost-hunters.com

"Haunted Ontario: Fort Erie," from Haunted Ontario, www.hauntedontario.com

"William Quantrill: Renegade Leader of the Missouri Border War," from www.legendsofamerica.com.

About the Author

Mary Beth Crain is an established journalist, editor, and author whose memoir, *A Widow, a Chihuahua and Harry Truman* (HarperSanFrancisco, 2000), was a *Los Angeles Times* bestseller. Her book *Guardian Angels* (Running Press, 2004) has sold over 150,000 copies and she also co-authored, with Terry Lynn Taylor, the bestselling *Angel Wisdom, The Optimystics Handbook,* and *Angel Courage* (all published by HarperSanFrancisco).

Crain co-wrote *The Tao of Negotiation* with Joel Edelman (Harper Collins/Business) and was the editor of *The Best of L.A.* (Chronicle Books). She is currently a contributing writer for the *L.A. Weekly* and the *Oceana Herald-Journal,* and the senior editor of *SOMA Review,* a popular online magazine featuring provocative and irreverent articles on religion and culture.

An avid fan of the paranormal, with a few ghost stories of her own to tell, Crain is currently working on a novel with a supernatural twist.